A Realm of Wind and Rain

Krystal Harding

KRYSTAL HARDING

A REALM OF WIND AND RAIN

CONTENTS

DEDICATION

To all those who grew up too early in life.

This is your sign not to give up.

A Note from the Author

Dear readers,

A Realm of Wind and Rain is an adult fantasy novel. The novel includes mature themes and is intended for readers 18+. This book contains content that may trigger some readers.

This book contains explicit sexual content, fantasy gore and violence, blood and suggestions of mental familial abuse and sexual and mental abuse in past relationships. Please read with caution. If books that have strong female leads who don't need men bother you, this series might not be for you. If you are against females with multiple male mates bothers you, this might not be the book for you. If you don't like banter, spice and open-door romance, this book might not be for you.

If none of the above bothers you, then you might've found the perfect book for you. A strong FMC who isn't afraid to stand her ground and fight for what she believes in is at the center of this epic fantasy. Her life is unfolding before your eyes, from love, learning to forgive, and searching for answers, all while finding herself along the way.

I hope you enjoy this series as much as I enjoyed writing it for you all. Enjoy—

Welcome to Cerulia

Krystal Harding

CHAPTER 1
LUNA

The crunch of the dry leaves beneath my boots was loud enough to make my ears ring. We've been walking for three days now, not a single deer or bear to be seen. Luther was grumbling about something; pretty sure he was just complaining about the cold. Even though autumn had just begun, the wind up here in the mountains makes me think we're going to have a cold winter and that it will be upon us sooner than usual. The pack that I've been carrying with me has been slowing my steps, granted my brother is taller so his steps are much wider, but damn he could at least help me with the pack once in a while.

"Hey! Slow down! I'm carrying a lot here!" I shouted at my brother, who was still trekking on as if I said nothing. I kneeled down and picked up a pebble, and chucked it at his head. Direct hit. He spun around, glaring at me. "I said slow down." I stuck my tongue out at him.

"I didn't hear you Luna. You should've spoken over the wind, not through it." He stopped and waited for me to catch up. I dropped the pack from my back and pulled out the canteen of water and drank greedily. "Here, I'll take the pack." Luther reached down to zip it back up and hauled it over his shoulder like he was hauling a small child. I offered him the canteen, but he just shook his head. I closed it back up and put it inside the side pouch. He began walking again.

We needed to find food soon. Hopefully, a deer, but I'd just be happy for a rabbit at this point. The bread and cheese we packed would probably last another day if we rationed it outright, but then we would have to return. Returning empty-handed wouldn't go well for our sick father and sister.

There was plenty that needed to be done at home, shopping, going to the market, and selling whatever pelts we could find. I had a few paintings that were drying when I left. Maybe the art gallery would be interested or maybe even one of the local nobles. We weren't poor, but we weren't rich either. Things were definitely tighter now than they were before.

I sighed, looking up at the sky through the trees. It was going to be nightfall soon and we would have to stop again. If we don't find a big game soon, we are going to need to settle soon. I wasn't a fan of that idea. I glanced ahead at Luther. He could go on and on in these mountains if he didn't have to return home. I think he would like that, though.

I tried to focus on what needed to be done. Get game, get home, and restart my responsibilities all over again. Another deep sigh grumbled out of me. I seriously hate being the one to take care of everyone and everything, but I guess I should be grateful that I live in one of the nicer houses closer to the market and that we live in Celvenia and not Galbranth. The slums there were horrible. The taverns are always filled with soldiers and ladies of the night. That was one way to make money that I shouldn't judge. To each their own, I guess.

I kept walking behind Luther, not really focusing on the ground, which I probably should've. My foot kicked under a tree root and down I went. I put my hands out to catch me, so I didn't bust my face open on the hard dirt path.

"You okay back there? Or did your klutzy self fall again?" Luther called back to me, but of course, he didn't stop.

I picked myself up and brushed my hands on my pants. Yup, definitely going to be a long day.

CHAPTER 2
LUNA

Rustling came from the bush up ahead, and I looked at Luther. He must not have heard it. I had my bow, now free, on my back with the pack no longer concealing it, in my hands within seconds, an arrow knocked in place. I dropped behind the mulberry bush to my left. I had to get this, even if it was something small, like a chipmunk or a squirrel.

Anything was better than nothing at this point. Green eyes glinted at me through the bush ahead. Did it see me? Some more rustling came than a bright orange fox with jade green eyes came into view. Perfect. I took aim at the fox, slowing my breath to a steady my hand. This was it. I took a deep breath and let my arrow fly true. I heard the wood pierce the flesh before I saw what I did. I hit an animal alright, but not the fox I was intending on getting, no that fox was gone and in its place was a mountain lion. Was it chasing the fox? How did we not see it? Either way, I got us food.

Climbing out from behind the bush, I yelled to Luther, "I got one!" He spun around and came running back to where I was standing. His bright green eyes widened as he saw the arrow sticking out the hide of the tan mountain lion I had shot. I wasn't going to tell him I meant to hit a fox. He wouldn't let me live it down that I missed my intended target. He kneeled down to check the lion and make sure the hide could be saved along with the meat.

"Good job. Clean kill, precise and accurate. I'm not surprised though, since you've been training more and more recently." Luther smiled at me like he was stating something I was trying to keep secret. Surprising enough, that wasn't the case. I grow tired of sitting around the house tending to Lilly and our father like I'm a nurse. I want to be free in the woods, running barefoot through the streams. Who cares if I step on a sharp stone and cut up my feet? To feel the moss under my feet, the wind in my face; that's the dream. He wouldn't get it though. He was always out in the woods, and further with the damn Fae's constant usage of us humans as soldiers. Not a damn one of them would fight for our lives, but we're expected to fight for theirs. It's not fair.

"Are we going to take it home and clean it or just do it here to make it easier to carry back? There's some potar leaves we can wrap the meat in over there." I pointed at the thick, wide, oval green leaves that grew it large patches around the woods. Potar plants had a nice earthy smell to them, like the smell of the air after a rainstorm. They were the perfect shape and size to wrap the meat in and we had plenty of string in the pack.

"That sounds like a smart plan. Did you pack the storage bag in the pack before we left?" Luther pulled out his knife, an obsidian serrated blade with a bone white elk antler handle that he handmade himself. I grabbed the pack and pulled out the grey storage bag, the thing was big enough to carry not just the meat from the mountain lion but probably that fox, maybe a rabbit too. I put the bag down by his side and he was examining the best spot to begin skinning the lion. "Can you go get a bunch of those leaves, we're gonna need a good amount." I nodded at him and just walked over to the thicket of potars. I pulled out my own obsidian blade and began to slowly cut the leaves from the base of the stems. If you cut them instead of just ripping them off, the potar plant would regrow the leaves from the same spot where you cut the original leaves from. It was such a beautiful plant. Sometimes if you got here right at dawn, you would be able to see it flower the most beautiful pinkish red flowers that smell like honey.

I brought back about a dozen leaves. Hopefully, this is enough for him. Luther finally had the animal skinned and was working on the meat and bones. I could tell he was weighing each bone mentally, wondering if it would be good to keep for making weapons from it. He was a bloody mess. "Do you want me to help you?" I asked from beside him. He barely grunted in acknowledgement to my question. I kneeled down beside him and started wrapping the bloody pieces of meat in the leaves, wrapping them with the twine from the pack.

Together we worked in silence, the usual way we worked, if I was being honest with myself. Quiet and efficient. I think he worries the Fae might find me more interesting than just a servant or housekeeper, that they would end up putting me in armor like him or in their beds.

I folded the hide flesh side on itself and wrapped it in the twine as well. It was getting dark out. Looks like we are making came again. At least tonight we wouldn't be hungry, and we could actually eat something with substance other than berries or stale cheese and bread.

I packed away the meat and hide in the storage bag and began pulling out the tent and bedrolls. Luther's was just a thick sheet at this point. Mine, however, was a little thicker since it only got used during our hunting trips.

"I'll make a fire and cook up some of the hind meat. We should be good for tonight. There's a stream up the ways. I'm going to go clean up first and refill the canteen." He grabbed the canteen out of the side of the pack where I placed it earlier and stalked off down the path towards the stream. Sighing, I started gathering sticks and logs from around the trees.

CHAPTER 3

LUTHER

*S*he's going to be bring me to shame if she keeps getting better. *What a bow and arrow,* I thought to myself as I walked towards the stream. My skin was cracking from the dried blood on me. I should've thought that through before, just ripping into the animal, but I wasn't thinking. I wanted to just get it gutted and cleaned and broken down before the deep setting set in and I had to break bones to move the animal.

Damn, she drank a lot more water than I realized. Maybe I should've taken the pack this morning. She has been carrying since yesterday. Ah! I'm such an asshole. I'll just carry that and the animal meat on the way back home. Goddess above strike me where I stand if I forget that in the morning.

I could hear the stream water rippling off the stones under the surface, the smell of the moss and water coated the air. Pushing back the last bit of brush before me, I could see the clear mirror like water in front of me. I'm gonna have to tell Luna to come up here and get cleaned up. I walked over to the stream and kneeled down, staring back at myself, my light brown hair now matted with blood, great I didn't want to get my hair wet, but I have no choice now. I washed my hands and the outside of the canteen together. Luckily, the stream was flowing south down the mountain. Fresh mountain water was the best to drink. Opening the canteen, I dunk the bottle into the water and let it fill up all the way before pulling it out. I recapped it and set it to the side. Using my hands, I made a cup and drank directly from the stream. Crisp, clean mountain water, no better way to describe the freshness to it.

There had to be some salmon upstream a little farther. Maybe in the morning I'll go up north a little ways and try to get some fish to bring home. Salmon fetches a high price back home. It would definitely be worth it.

I didn't want to get fully in the water but screw it; I need to get this blood off of me. I kicked off my boots and untied my knife from my belt and left them by the shore. Tugging off the grey shirt and brown pants i was wearing, I dunked them into the water to clean them. Thank gods Luna was down by the tent; I don't want her to see me like this. Dunking my head under the water, I scrubbed my hair and beard. Fingers snagging on dried blood and knots. I really need to get a brush through my hair when I get back to camp. I emerged from the water and wiped my eyes; it wasn't a cold evening, but the air made my wet body prickle with goosebumps. I walked my way out of the stream, trying to avoid slipping on the wet rocky stream bed. Time to shake this water off, get dressed and head back.

Slipping back into my mostly soaked clothes and my dry boots, I grabbed the canteen and my knife off the shore and started my walk back towards the camp. It was peaceful here, and a much-needed break from the loudness of the war camps. Why in the world King Harold wanted to continue to fight these petty wars was beyond my pay grade, but if helps keep my family sheltered and mostly fed so I guess I should be grateful. I just hate senseless violence. I saw Luna through the trees, her blonde and blue hair a dead giveaway that she was someone special. Her bright brown eyes were squinting at the bushes across from where she sat by a high pile of logs and sticks. The simple green shirt and tan leggings hugged onto her ample body as if they were a size too small for her frame. I needed to get her better clothes and better boots when I get back to town. I'm definitely going to go fishing in the morning.

"The stream's free if you want to go wash up. I filled the canteen too." I pushed through the last of the thick grass back into the makeshift campsite. Impressed that, she got the tent set up and the bed rolls out. "I'll get the fire going and

I'll start on cooking up 2 of the smaller steaks."

"Okay, do you want my brush?" She smiled at me, extending her hair brush towards me. I nodded and grabbed it from her and began roughly pulling it through my hair, gods it felt like my hair was straw. She winced as she heard the knots being ripped out of my hair. I ran the brush quickly through my beard and pulled out my hair from around the bristles before returning it to her. "You're going to be bald before your 30 if you keep ripping that brush through your hair like that." She took the brush from me and returned it to the pack.

"Go get cleaned up," I said, ruffling her hair as I walked past her to the firewood. Cooking these steaks on an open fire with no skillet was going to be interesting. She huffed at me but grabbed her knife, tied it to a makeshift belt and headed into the woods from where I just came.

Luna

I keep feeling like someone is following me, like I'm being stared at. Looking around, I don't see anyone there. The only footsteps seem to be my own. Luther doesn't have fae sight, so I know it isn't his eyes that I feel watching me. Sighing, I resign the thought to the back of my head and push forward through the thick grass and the potar plants. I could smell the stream before I saw it, the moss, the wet grass, the slight smell of fish coming from the northern part of the stream. It was a heavenly scent, if I was being honest. The subtle scent of apples filled the air, which was odd since there weren't any apple trees this far up in the mountains. Ignoring the slight warning bells in my head, I stroll over to the side of the stream and glance down at the crystal-clear water flowing down the mountains and towards the town below. Yeah, I was a covered in dirt and desperately needed to wash my face.

I pulled my boots off gently, my feet aching from the hike these past few days. I tugged off my makeshift rope belt, freeing my knife from the monstrosity I created and set it inside my left boot. I stripped off my green cotton shirt and my fleece tan leggings and socks and folded them neatly, placing them all in a small pile next to the edge of the stream. My undergarments, as simple as they are, were quite comfortable, but I was definitely keeping them on.

Wading my way into the stream, I glanced around once more to see if I might be visited by another of the villagers up here hunting as well. Luther and I were the only two who came this far up not afraid of the children's stories as the others in town. *The Fae will come and steal you away if you are out in their homelands for more than 3 days.* What silly nonsense. The fae only saw us as slaves, tools to be used for their needs. Nothing more and nothing less. Our father was one believer of this child's tale and refuses to let us be out longer than 3 days. Tomorrow will mark our 4th day on the hike. As long as we are back in town before nightfall, he won't lose his mind on us.

The water was nice and cool, not freezing, but not extremely hot. It was perfect. I tied up my long hair using a free strand to wrap it up and hold it in place. I rather wash it when I get home than let it get wet for no reason. It was beautiful out here and so peaceful. Slowly, I lowered myself down into the water until it was up to my collarbone and closed my eyes. It felt so good to be in the water again. We used to swim in Lake Gilder by Mirith when we were kids all the time. I missed the warm waters there, always bubbling softly thanks to the natural hot springs beneath it. Or at least that's what mom used to tell us. I missed mom wherever she is. I hope she's happy and healthy. A splash from down the stream had my eyes flying open and searching. What the hell was that? Looking down the stream, I couldn't see anything, it's probably just a fish. I had to calm my nerves down. I have no idea why I'm so anxious.

Looking back towards where I heard the splash, I saw a streak of what looked like orange swiftly moving through the water. Blinking my eyes and rubbing them furiously, I had to look again to make sure I wasn't seeing things. Nothing was there. I need to just finish rinsing off and get the hell back to camp before the night fully takes hold. Quickly, I gently scrubbed at my fingers and my arms with nothing but the water, making the water a cloudy mess around me. When I get home, the shower and I are going to be having a long meeting. I made my way back to the shore and let my body air dry just a little before putting my clothes back on. I think I have a long shirt in the bag I can wear tonight so everything can dry overnight. I retied the makeshift belt around my waist and made sure my knife was secure and started the walk back to the campsite. Luther should've gotten the fire started by now. Hopefully, he didn't overcook the steaks. I'm not one of his army buddies who likes shoe leather.

CHAPTER 4
LUNA

The fire was roaring a beautiful orange, red and yellow by the time I reached the campsite. Well, good, he got that done. Walking past the tent, I noticed the pack had been thoroughly ransacked. He must've been looking for something to use as silverware and gave up. I bent down and picked up the pack and started repacking, so everything actually got put away and didn't get left out overnight like he does from time to time.

"I was gonna take care of that in the morning. Come, eat." Luther pointed to a potar leaf with a slender piece of meat cut up on it. Setting the pack down, I made my way over to the log. He turned into seating and picked up the leaf. Heavy and sturdy, despite looking like it was the thinnest thing on the planet. The steak smelled heavenly, and it surprisingly wasn't overcooked. I smiled at my brother. As much of a pain in the ass as he is, he always worries about me and makes sure that I eat and have what I need. Lilly would've loved tonight. I wonder if she went outside today to get some fresh air. When we got home, I am definitely taking her outside to paint.

I guess the look on my face went from happy to somber because Luther looked at me with utter concern all over his face. "I'm fine," I said, looking down at the makeshift plate on my lap, "I just miss Mom, and I'm worried about dad and Lilly."

"They will get better Luna. They will find out how to cure the graying and they will get better. Stay positive. As for Mom, she left us. You need to come to terms that we weren't as important to her as she was to us." Luther shoved an overcooked piece of meat in his mouth and chewed with aggression. He hated me bringing up Mom, but I don't think she just left us. There had to be a reason and Dad thought so too. If he wasn't sick, he would be out there looking for her still. Luther broke my silent thoughts raging in my head. "Sorry, I know you and Lilly were little when she left and you're allowed to miss her. I just wish she wouldn't have left the way she did."

"Do you really think she left us because she wanted to? Or do you think maybe, just maybe, she left to find a cure for Lilly?" I bit out the last question, a little harsher than I meant. I was allowed to be mad, though. He always spoke of mom like she was a villain in our lives. When she left us, she said she would return and make things better. I will always believe she will return to us and things will be better.

"I think mom didn't know how to handle the fact that her baby got the graying and couldn't face the possible loss of her. I think she selfishly left us to live a life where she wasn't duty bound to take care of a sick child. I don't think she could've stayed around any longer. And before you even say it, yes, she said she would return, but it's been ten years since then Luna. Ten long years you have raised Lilly. You were only twelve, and I was only sixteen. Neither of us should've had to grow up so fast. We had Dad, so yeah there was an adult to provide, but what did he do for Lilly except fill her head with the idea that Mom was searching for a cure for her? Lilly has given up hope that mom plans on coming home at all." Luther had a serious look on his face. He really held a grudge against mom.

I quickly finished my food and threw the leaf into the fire. I was done sitting with him and his moody self. "I'm going to bed." I announced as I got up and strode for the tent. He didn't bother to acknowledge me or even try to stop me. Guess he wants to stay in his crap mood all night. Fine by me, I wanted sleep. Today was tiring and I'm ready to just go to bed.

A set of jeweled green eyes and a long orangish snout pushed into the tent. Looking at her like this felt wrong. I should advert my eyes and give her the respect she deserves, but why do I want to be around her? Why the hell did I let her almost shoot me with an arrow?! Seriously, there is something wrong with my brain. But at least she shot that mountain lion before it ate me. I nudged further into the tent. The big brute who came to Wardveil with her was snoring so loudly outside the tent it was a miracle she could even sleep at all.

She looks peaceful, more so than she did in the stream. Stupid salmon splashing around made her hurry out of the water. I should've looked away, I shouldn't have stared, but by the goddess, she is so lovely. Her body was perfection, slightly thick around the hips and thighs, a plush tummy, ample gorgeous breasts, and a backside that I would love to use as a pillow. I've seen Fae women of all shapes and sizes and yet none of them compared to the human girl before me.

Looking around the tent, I notice the secondary bed roll laid out on the other side of the small, cramped tent. Must be for the brute outside. Are they together? They smell of each other, but that could be for a multitude of reasons. *Don't jump to conclusions Fennik, you don't know who he is to her. You are only interested in her because she's not like the other humans who come here and you're only curious to know what makes her different?* I hate it when my brain has to remind me of things. I wish I had my shoulder bag; my notebook and pens would be very useful to detail my interaction with her while she sleeps.

Rustling and a faint whimper came from outside the tent, and I knew that damn whimper. If I don't leave now, he will come in here and either hurt her or drag me out by my tail. I take one more look at her and inhale deeply. I'll come back in the morning to make sure she's safe.

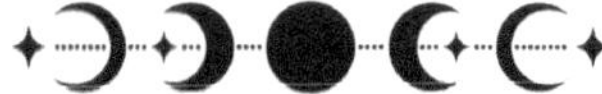

Sunlight and the song of the gait birds filtered into the small, cramped tent. Why did they have to be so loud? Rolling over to look towards where Luther should be asleep, I jump up, realizing he's not in the tent. Did he leave me last night after our talk? Dread settled in until the rumbling snore of what sounded like a grizzly bear filled the air. He slept outside. Relief washed over me as I realized he was still here. I rolled off the bedroll and felt something fuzzy under my palms. I looked down to see what looked like orange fur covering my bed roll like I was sleeping with an animal.

I moved off the bedroll and leaned over towards Luther's and rolled them both up. Maybe I had the fur on me from laying on the ground. Maybe it was under my bedroll, and I didn't notice it when I set it up last night. Of course, that had to be the only logical reasoning behind it.

I stepped outside the tent and took a deep breath, stretching my arms and legs from sleeping on the ground all night. I cannot wait to get home and into my bed. My friends back home all thought I was nuts for coming up here. Kira and Harper would definitely have a few words to say to me when I got home. I just need to get this tent packed up and put away, then we can get the hell out of here. Slowly, I dismantled the tent and fold it into a tight bundle that will fit in the pack. I grabbed up the pack and dropped it on Luther's stomach. He grunted as his eyes flew open, knife in hand, ready to pounce until he realized it was little old me. I stuck my tongue out at him and turned around to walk away. He could carry everything today. I wasn't about to help him carry everything after how he talked about mom last night.

"Mad at me or something?" Luther yelled at me from his sleeping spot on the ground.

I spun around and faced him, anger rippling across my face. "What do you think?!" I snarled at him. "You make it seem like mom was so horrible to us, but she wasn't! You chose not to be around for the last year. That's on you, not on her. So stop saying she left us because she couldn't handle life with a sick kid!"

He looked at me, completely dumbfounded, like I had just hit him in the face with a brick. And well, I guess I kinda did, but I don't care. He needs to hear how he sounds. I turned away from him and quickly caught the flash of orange and white in the berry bushes ahead of where I stood. I grabbed my bow and quiver full of arrows and headed toward the colors. "Go catch your stupid salmon. I'm gonna hunt my way back down the mountain!" I shouted over my shoulder at Luther, then sprinted off down the path. He shouted something at me, but I threw up a vulgar gesture at him from behind. I was going to catch that fox if it was the last thing I did on this hike.

I should've grabbed the damn pack. Definitely wasn't thinking about sleeping arrangements on the way back. It took us three days to get to where we stopped. If I don't stop as frequently and follow the stream, I should be able to get back home before nightfall tomorrow.

No sign of the fox I was following earlier. It must've realized I was closing in on it and scattered off somewhere. Maybe if I'm lucky, I'll catch some fish and be able to grill them up tonight over a fire. I still had my lighter in my pocket, so that would make things easier. I'd been walking for hours, and Luther hadn't caught up to me. I don't know if I'm more pissed that he isn't here or more relieved. Either way, I could do this on my own. The sun was setting, and I needed to make camp soon before I couldn't see. I'll sleep by the stream tonight, the view of the stars from there will be amazing. I headed through the trees and towards the stream. At this altitude the stream was coming down the mountain faster and made more sounds as the water tripped over bigger rocks. I started grabbing sticks and making a fire box, two sticks going north to south, then placing two more sticks on top of those going east to west and continued doing it until there was a decent amount of space between the ground and the top sticks. Grabbing some potar leaves, I placed them in the center of the stick, pulled out my lighter and said a silent prayer to Undas, the god of fire, that my idea would work.

Flick, flick, whoosh–the light lit and the potar leaves were a blaze. I looked to the skies and nodded my thanks. I set my bow and quiver down next to where I planned on building my fire. Fishing without a rod would be tough, but I had plenty of sticks around me and I could turn one into a mini spear using my knife to sharpen a point. I moved a slightly larger log over to the fire, grabbed and stick, unhooked my knife and dwindled down the tip, tossing the scraps into the fire. I was resourceful. Well, this was as good as it was going to get. Time to go fish hunting. I laughed to myself as I pictured Lilly trying to do this exact thing when we were younger, before she got sick. She fell into the water several times and ended up catching a trout in her skirts. I shook my head and tried to refocus my mind. I needed to eat, and soon by the sounds on my grumbling stomach.

I got to the edge of the stream and glanced down. Bright blues and reds flashed in the water. There were more fish downstream than what I expected. I kicked off my boots and socks and rolled my leggings up to my knees. I wouldn't need to go that far in. I grabbed the stick and walked into the water up to mid-calf. Steadying my breathing, I inhaled and slammed the spear straight down in front of me. It met some resistance, and I saw some red filtering into the water. Good, I think I got one. I pulled the spear out and saw that I stabbed what looked like a red gully. Perfect, this should be enough for me tonight. I walked back out of the stream and towards the fire. Fixing the gully on the spear, I dug the opposite edge of the spear into the ground and leaned it towards the fire to cook. I had to go grab my boots and socks.

Just as I turned around, I saw the flash of orange again. I grabbed my bow and knocked an arrow into place and aimed it at where my clothes were sitting. A fox was sitting right next to my boots, staring at me. How did I not hear it come near me? How long was it there? The fox grabbed my boots in its mouth and started walking towards me. Shock filled me as I kept my bow aimed directly at its head. Foxes could be rabid and could attack for no reason. But why in the world was it bringing me my boots? It dropped my boots at the edge of my campsite and sat there as if waiting for me to thank it. Releasing my grip on the bowstring gently, I set the arrow and bow next to me and gingerly crept towards my boots. Ever so slowly, I pulled my socks out of the boots and put them on, following with the boots. I kept my eyes on the fox.

"Are you hungry?" I asked the fox as if it would answer me. To my surprise, it looked like it nodded at me. "Well, if you want food, then you'll have to share with me. I only caught one gully."

I turned and reached over to rotate the fish, thankfully it didn't burn on the one side. I looked over at the fox, its green eyes assessing me. "Sorry for aiming my bow at you. Hunting, it's dangerous to be an animal when humans are hunting for food." I don't know why I was talking to the fox, but here I was.

The fox looked at me and I could swear it started smiling at me. Its fur started retreating and slowly began turning into pale flesh. My eyes grew wide as I watch the small fox turn into a gorgeous man right in front of me. His pale skin glowed in the firelight, his hair now a shaggy mess around his face. He smiled. If I had any sense in my head, I would be terrified. If I was smart, I would run because if there was anything to fear, it was the Fae male in front of me.

One of our masters. I should've known better.

"I figured it would be easier to answer your question if you could actually understand me." He smiled at me. He looked so young. "I would love to share the gully with you. Unless you would like me to go catch my own?"

I shook my head slightly to keep my jaw from dropping. "I can share. It's not like it's that small of a fish." I looked back at the fire. I can't believe I am talking to a Fae.

Gods, I am so stupid.

"What's your name? I would love to know who I am to thank for this generous deed." His voice was light, not loud or quiet, but easy on the ears. Like a gentle caress in my ears.

"My name is Luna, Luna Rayne Cromwell. May I ask who you are?" I asked, looking over at him again, "Hey wait, where did the clothes come from?"

"My name is Fennik," he laughed a bit. "And the clothes," he gestured down at his jade green shirt and tan pants, "Magic my dear Luna. It's all part of my magic." He looked at me like he wanted to devour me, and a part of me melted to my core. Oh, gods, how long had it been since I thought about doing *that*? I had to suppress the urge that my body was about to betray to him.

"Well, good, I'm glad you're not sitting here naked, because that would make this meeting very awkward. I'll finish cooking the fish in a moment. I need to go grab some potar leaves." I stood and walked over to the closest potar plant and gently cut off four leaves with my knife. I just needed to get this meal over with and maybe he would leave me alone for the night and go back to where ever he came from. Not that he wasn't attractive at or anything. Looking up to the sky, I cursed whatever god or goddess thought this might be funny and hugged the leaves to my chest as I walked back towards the fire. "Ok, these should do the trick." I grabbed the spear and placed the fish on top of a leaf, using another to act as a glove to help pull it off without burning my hands too badly. Fennik just sat there watching me pick apart the gully as if it was the most interesting thing he has ever seen. "Is something wrong?" I asked, to break his unblinking stare.

"Oh no, I'm sorry. I have a tendency to lose myself in the work of others. Do you cook often for yourself?" He asked all the world genuine. Not at all like most of the fae males that we've met over the years.

"Yes, actually I do. My mother left when I was 12, and my father couldn't really cook to save his life. So, I took up the cooking and cleaning of the house. My sister has the graying and now so does my father. So, it's up to me and my brother to hunt and cook and clean. But he fights in the wars that constantly keep happening, so it's mainly left to me to do it all." I stared down at the fish in my hands. I haven't spoken this aloud so freely with anyone other than Luther.

"That sounds like a lot for one person to take on. I'm sorry." Pity laced his words. I didn't want his pity. I wanted him to tell his kind to stop fighting with others and bring their healers to the human towns and help us. Our kind are dying for their kind. The least they could do is make sure we are healthy enough so we can fight for them. As if sensing my anger, Fennik spoke again, "I'm sorry if I offended you. My kind rarely speaks to your kind one on one like this. It's a shame because humans are very interesting beings. Ones I want to study and learn from. My kind have a tendency to see humans as tools for war or for other needs. Which isn't right and my brothers and I want that to change. But our father likes the old ways. So, for that I apologize."

"You're fine. I just don't speak so openly about my family to those I hardly know. Anyway, here. I hope it's enough for you." I hand him over the potar leaf with half the gully shredded on it. He took it ever so gently. His fingers brushed my fingertips and set a shiver up my arm and down my spine. I grabbed my leaf and dug into my food. It wasn't the best, but it was edible. Something clicked into place and my head.

CHAPTER 5
FENNIK

S hit, shit, shit! I said father and brothers, she must have just realized who I am. I looked up at her. The shock and realization in her eyes was weighing. Well, if I didn't doom myself before by shifting in front of her, I surely did with that sentence.

"Yes, I am Prince Fennik of the Autumn Realm. I apologize for not saying so sooner. But most humans wouldn't speak so kindly to me if they knew who I was." I set the leaf down on the ground. "Thank you for sharing your fish with me. I can catch you another if you'd like and then I'll leave you alone." I got up and turned towards the stream, ready for her to scream or yell at me, but I heard laughter. Like the sound of a beautiful symphony, I spun around to find her wiping her eyes. "Did I say something funny?"

"Not particularly. I'm just laughing at my luck. I almost shot you twice now and wouldn't that have caused a stir? Human woman killed Fae Prince. Yeah, someone would've had my head for that." She shook her head and went back to her meal. "You don't have to get me another one. Hell, you don't even have to leave."

Now it was my turn to have the look of shock and disbelief on my face. "Well, you probably would've gotten me if that mountain lion didn't jump in the way like it did. Grateful as I am to the lion, your skill had me kind of glued to the spot." I smiled and sat back down, picking up my leaf and finishing the last bit of the gully. It definitely needed salt, maybe even some pepper, but I was not about to complain about her kindness.

"Like I said, when Luther is away for the Kin- I mean, your father, I have to do the hunting myself. I wouldn't be any good at it if the animals could hear me a mile away or if I fumbled or delayed the kill. I'm sorry I tried to kill you." She threw her leaf into the fire. I followed suit.

"It's fine. You're not the first person to take aim at me, be it with a sword, an arrow, or a spear." I chuckled. "But never by someone as pretty as you." I tried to smile at her to make her feel at ease, and I hoped she wouldn't take that spear and chuck it at my head. Instead, she just stared into the fire, using her spear to shift the logs and sticks. "I'm assuming the man you were with is your brother, Luther?"

"Yeah, I left him this morning. We had a bit of a fight last night. I don't really want to talk about it. I have a long walk back to Celvenia tomorrow. I want to get home before my father realizes we've been gone for over three days. He believes the stupid children's stories about your kind kidnapping humans who are in Mistward and the

Mitos Mountains for over three days." She shrugged and looked up at the stars.

"There are really stories told about us like that?" I said in full disbelief. We would never kidnap humans. Most just die from being ill prepared or from falling off cliffs. To blame the fae must be easier than admitting that their kind is flawed. She nodded. "Well, that isn't true. You seem like a woman with a good head on your shoulders. If we wanted to kidnap your kind, we wouldn't wait for three days. Plus, if that was the case, wouldn't you and your brother have been kidnapped by now?"

"I don't believe in the stories, and Luther is just fearless. He thinks being a part of the army makes him immune to death. Honestly, I think he's just reckless. My father and sister, however, believe. I just wish a fae would kidnap me and get me away from my life sometimes." She looked at me and put her hands up. "I don't actually want to be kidnapped." She smiled and looked back up at the sky. "Sometimes life is just hard, and you question what god or goddess finds humor in your misery."

"I get that. I'm the youngest of five brothers. I've been told one day my curiosity will get me killed. Hell, my brother Damian was out here last night checking on me because he was hunting north of your campsite and smelled the blood." She looked at me, a flash of terror hit her eyes. "No worries, he looks like a beast from Hellis but he's practically a puppy."

If Damian heard me call him a puppy, I would probably be getting thumped right on the head. However, I didn't want her to fear us. And by the look in her eyes, she already did. "Can I ask you something Luna?" She looked at me and nodded. "Why are you so afraid of my kind? It has to be more than just the wars. Did something happen to you? Did one of my kind hurt you?" Hoping the seriousness in my voice would make her answer honestly.

"I told you my father and sister have the graying and my mother left. She was trying to find a fae lord she worked in service for when she was younger. He was said to have powerful healers who could heal any sickness. It's been 10 years and we haven't seen or heard from her. Luther and my father think she used it as an excuse to get away from a sick child. I believe that she's out there still trying to find help. Lilly has given up waiting for a cure and just wishes nightly that the graying will take her in her sleep. The coughing is getting worse, she can't keep anything down half the time. It's a lot to handle. She tried to stop taking the tonics from the local physicians, but they do little except for calm the coughing fits. Nothing more. The Fae have healers, but they won't send any to help heal the villagers they use for war. It's like we are little more than lesser beings to them. Expendable for wars, useful in the bedroom and to tidy their homes and gardens, but nothing more than that." Her gaze went hollow, and my heart ached for her. So much sadness and sorrow in such a short lifetime.

"Do you know the Lord whom your mother is looking for? I might be able to help. Even if not, we have our own healers close by. Maybe I could see if one would be so kind as to leave their home to come see to your father and sister." My offer was genuine. Luna had a point. Our kind used humans like humans used toilet paper. One use and then discarded. Hearing it from her lips broke me. She finally looked at me with tears in her eyes.

"I don't think my family would let your healer in the door sadly. My father hates the fae. He blames them for my mother leaving us, and my sister is just done fighting. Luther, well, he is a soldier and will do as he's commanded, but the fae don't demand entrance into our homes. It wouldn't look right. But thank you." She laid back on the hard ground and closed her eyes.

"I'll still see if maybe they'll make a tonic that I can bring to you. Even if we just meet in the woods by the stream right outside the town gates. It's the least I can do to repay your kindness to me." I practically whispered it into the wind. Her chest rose and fell softly, her eyes shifting beneath the lids. She had fallen asleep. I laid back on the ground myself. It wasn't the most comfortable while in my fae form, and if I wasn't comfortable, she couldn't be comfortable.

Well, here goes nothing. I started my shift, but not into the fox that she would know, but my other form, my true form. Orange reddish fur spread over my body, bones cracking and shifting into place, a long snout replacing where my nose and mouth once were. My wolf's form was large, but the fur was softer. I walked over to where Luna was sleeping and nudged her softly with my nose. She looked at me through sleep eyes and I just laid down around her; she curled up into me and fell back to sleep. Hopefully, she wouldn't wake up and try to kill me.

CHAPTER 6
LUNA

The sun was just starting its journey across the pinkish blue sky; I tried to recollect the events from last night. Why did I tell him about my family? And why wasn't I afraid of him? He reminds me of Lord Drake. Kind, gentle, and sweet. The thoughts ran through my head and the more I thought about it, the more my head hurt. I stretched my arms and felt fur touch my palms.

I opened my eyes, expecting to see a Fox, but no, that was definitely not what was beside me. A giant orange and reddish wolf lay there curled in a ball, sound asleep. I grabbed my bow and quiver and slowly backed away into the trees behind me. If that isn't Fennik, I'm not about to be its lunch. I dropped behind a blackberry bush and searched the ground for a pebble or stick. My hand scraped against a sharp small stone, and I picked it up. I looked over at the wolf and prayed I wasn't about to make a mistake. I chucked the stone as hard as I could at the wolf. Its head perked up, and it looked around the area. Within a blink of my eyes, Fennik changed back into his Fae form, but this time he had much less covering his upper body.

"I'm sorry!" I shouted from the bushes. He put his hands up and smiled.

"Don't shoot! I'm harmless, I promise." He lowered his hands as I crawled out of the bush. "At least you threw a rock and not an arrow." He chuckled.

"So, you can change into more than just a fox?" I asked, my interest piqued. He shrugged as he ran his hand through his knotted orange hair.

"Only a Fox and a wolf. Most fae have two forms. Some, if they're strong enough, can shift into about four different creatures. Comes in handy when I need to get away faster. My wolf can cover more ground." He looked at me with a wicked grin on his face and it made me nervous. "I have an idea."

"I don't like that you looked as if you want to eat me." I shook my head at him as I slowly backed away.

"I promise I will not eat you Luna. I just know you said your father is gonna be mad when he realizes how long you've been gone. I can carry you in my wolf's form back to the edge of the forest. I obviously won't take you straight home, but at least you'll get home in time." He waited there, watching me, waiting for me to make my decision. It would be easier to get home if he helped me. And considering all his kind has done to my people, about time they do something for me.

"Alright, on one condition," he nodded, waiting patiently. "Leave me at the fork in the paths, but the sapphire blooms. It's about a ten-minute walk to town from there, but deep enough in that you won't be seen."

He considered what I had said. The sapphire blooms were my favorite type of roses, so I wasn't planning ongoing straight home. But he didn't need to know that.

"Alright, that sounds like a plan. Want to leave now?" He asked. I nodded my head and before I could say anything else, he shifted back into that humongous wolf. He lowered his body so I could climb on. I slung my bow and quiver over my back and tried gently to get on his back. I am nowhere on the thin side, more so the cuddly plush, but I still don't want to hurt him.

He hoisted me up with one small jump and off we were going. Straight down the mountain, following the stream. The colors of greens and blues and whites blurred together. I hugged onto his neck to keep myself in place. I must've been hugging a little too tight because he slowed his pace. Maybe he just forgot I was there. The town was coming into a larger view. The tall stone walls surrounding the town made it look it a prison. Soldiers guarded the iron bar gates in their shiny silver armor. Only the Captains and Generals wore the signature blue capes. Fennik slowed his pace, the sun now higher in the sky. I hadn't realized how long we had been going for or even how fast he was running. He got to the fork in the path by the Sapphire Blooms and leaned down, brushing his belly to the grass. I slid off as gracefully as I could manage. He walked off into the bushes a wolf and strode back out a fully clothed male. His green suit looked like it had just been ironed, his messy orange hair ruffled. He looked like something straight out of a fantasy novel and acted like a prince from one to.

"Thank you for the ride. Sorry if I was squeezing you a little too tight." I smiled but looked down at my feet, wringing my hands in front of me like some school girl talking to her crush. What the hell was wrong with me?

"You were fine. I'm just not used to someone riding on my back. I forgot you were there and that I should've been slower for you." He grabbed my hand and planted a kiss on the back of my right hand. "It was a pleasure to meet you Luna Rayne. Meet me here tomorrow evening just as the lightning bugs dance. I should have something to help your sister and father. Just don't tell them where it came from." He smiled, dropped my hand, and placed his own in his pants pockets. "Until tomorrow evening, my dear. Farewell."

He vanished before I could say thank you. I turned down the left of the path and started walking back home.

CHAPTER 7
LUNA

"Father I'm home." I called as I entered the two-story stone house. The wooden floorboards groaned under my boots. The smell of the pine trees in the backyard wafted through the open windows. I could also smell a weird scent, like cinnamon and cloves. That's odd, we don't have those things yet. Not since we haven't been able to go to the market. Just as I kicked my boots off at the doorway and walked four steps into the house, auburn hair caught my attention. "Harper!" The ivory skinned woman was sitting in my usual seat by the window, humming a beautiful little tune.

"Welcome home Luna." Harper chimed as she got up from the chair and glided across the floor to me. She embraced me in what some might call a brute hug, but she was always strong. She had to be, considering she and her sister Kaia were dual leads in the theater by the town square. "Where is Luther? Wasn't he with you?"

I waved her off. "Luther was being a prick, so I left him in the mountains. He's strong. He'll be fine." I walked over to the kitchen and grabbed a cup from the cupboard. He would be fine I reminded myself. He was trained for that kind of thing; I grabbed the pitcher of tea from the fridge. "How are they today? Any better?"

She looked at me with sadness in her eyes, "Lilly won't leave her bed, and your father has been sleeping nonstop for the last 2 days. I tried to wake him up, but he just waves myself or Kaia off. Virgil even tried to wake him this morning and he about threw a book at him."

"I appreciate you guys helping out. It means a lot to me to have such great friends." I took a sip of the tea, definitely made by Kaia. Super sweet with a hint of hibiscus. I set the cup down and looked at Harper but before I could even open my mouth the door flung open, and Luther was in the doorway seething at me. "You look pissed."

"I had to carry both packs down the damn mountain all by myself you spoiled brat!" He spat out at me as he tossed the bag full of meat and what smelled like fish on the table.

"Smells like you took my advice to go catch some fish. I had no luck with finding anymore red meat, but I did spear a fish last night to eat." I grinned at him. Oh, he was pissed alright but I did not care. He deserved what he got. Harper shot me a wary glance.

"I think I'll leave you two to have at it. Kira and I have rehearsal tonight for the recital two days from now. I'm glad you made it back in time for it. Kira would've went into the mountains to hunt you down herself if you weren't back by morning." Harper gave me one last hug and left me with Luther.

"Do you have any idea what was going through my mind on my way home when I couldn't find you on any of the paths?" Luther's' blue eyes were like a storm raging in the sea. I felt bad but I stood my ground.

"Does it matter? We aren't on the same page, and I wasn't about to deal with you being a miserable prick the whole hike back. I made it home in one piece following the stream. I'm not some useless child." I tried not to raise my voice.

The door to fathers room opened and out walked a stunning blonde haired, blue eyes man, his muscles straining the grey shirt he was wearing. "You two can be so loud some days." He said as he walked out of the room closing the door behind him. The tattooed arms flexed as he put some restraint in his grasp from slamming the door by accident. Virgil was a tall man, ripped honestly, an easy on the eyes. I couldn't help by drop my gaze to his hips. Luther didn't know but Virgil was my first when I was eighteen and he would probably kill him if he did know. But alas he was just a fling, and we hadn't been together since. Not for lack of wanting but Luther wouldn't let us be alone once Virgil made a comment about my ass.

"Hi, Virgil," I smiled and threw my arms around him in a hug. His calloused hands gripped me in return, slowly running up and down my spine. Gods, this man would be my undoing.

"Hello kitten," he purred in my ear so Luther couldn't hear. He smiled down at me and reluctantly let me out of his arms so he could go to my brother. "Luther." He clasped hands with my brother in the most stereotypical bro hug I have ever seen. Virgil needed a haircut, his normally kept short bald fade was more than a few weeks over done. I guess I'll have to add that to my list of things to do now that I'm home.

"How is he?" Luther looked at Virgil, who shook his head.

"It's not good. I mean, yeah, he threatened to beat me with a book, but he's been sleeping more often than he is awake. I don't want to say that it's looking grim but-" he trailed off, not finishing his sentence. Luther dropped his head. The look of defeat all settled into his features.

"What if we could get to the healers of Mistveil and ask them for help? They're not opposed to helping humans. They're just against leaving their home. Maybe one of us could go get help." I said from the counter. Which was apparently the worst thing I could've said. Luther gripped the chair from the table and flung it against the wall next to me. I screamed and Virgil was in front of me in a blink of an eye, his knife out and in his hand.

"You want to abandon us like she did! You're no better than her if you leave us. You have a duty to this family and it's about time you remember that." Luther stalked towards me, but Virgil held his ground.

"I do more for this family than you do! I take care of our sick sister and father while you're away in Galbranth whoring yourself out when you're not out fighting. I hunt when you're here and when you're away. I cook, I clean, I do your laundry, I take care of those I shouldn't have to! Our father did the same shit as you and put everything on me. Lilly is our sister, not our child, yet I've raised her. Not you, not father and not mother. So, kiss my ass, you ungrateful shit!" I slammed past Virgil and spit directly in Luther's face before grabbing my boots and storming out of the house. I could hear them arguing in the house, but I didn't care. I'm going to find a healer and help my family. Screw Luther.

VIRGIL

I saw red; I wanted to kill him. "How dare you talk to her like that!" I spat between clenched teeth. "She has done everything for your family, for you and hell. She's even taken care of me when we've come back here after drunken nights out that saw us brawling others. Not once did she complain. Not once has she asked for any semblance of her own freedom or life. You take her for granted." Clenching my fist tight around the bone handle of my knife, I wanted to hit him.

"Yeah, you're right. She has done a lot for you, hasn't she? Following you around like a lost puppy to its master." He had the nerve to smile at me. Arrogant, bastard.

"Well, maybe if you were such a prick she would've told you by now," I clipped my knife back in its sheath and leaned over the table to look him in the eyes, "I was her first."

The shocked expression on his face was enough for me to regret the words I had just said. He truly didn't know. Before I could open my mouth, a hard blow back at my jaw. The world shook, but it was on. I swung right at his face, connecting my right fist to his temple. He stumbled back, and I swept my leg out, taking him down by his knees. He should've known better than to have hit me first. I pounced, landing on top of him, throwing blow for blow on his ribs, his face and his chest. He would regret making her cry. But then I heard it.

A soft sudden gasp came from the hallway, my eyes shooting up to find Lilly holding onto the corner of the wall to keep herself upright. I messed up big time. I got off Luther and walked to where Lily was standing. Her thin frame and short brown hair showed just what the greying could do to someone. Her chocolate browns eyes, Luna's eyes, were dull, not the shining eyes she had when she was a kid. Luna had a point, and Luther needed to let it go. A healer could help Lilly and Gunther and let Luna live the life she deserved. "Lily, come on, let's get you back to bed."

"Is Luna made at me?" Lily's voice was barely above a whisper. It broke me each time I heard her speak.

"No of course not. Luther said some not so nice things to her. She's not mad at you, she's mad at him." I shot him a look. He was climbing up off his knees wiping blood from his mouth. Good. "Come on, I'll get you some tea."

Lilly twisted out of my reach and looked right at Luther. "She deserves to be happy, Luther. You're not nice to her like you are to me. Neither is Father. If I die, she won't stay around for you or Father." Lilly knew her words would cut me like a knife at each blow landed as I watched Luther sink into a chair by the table and watched Lilly walk back down the hallway. I followed her. "I hope the greying takes me soon, Virgil. And when it does," she glanced at me with hope in her eyes, "Take her away from here and away from them."

We walked into her room; I grabbed her hand and knelt on one knee. "I promise you will live, and I will get both of you out of here." She laid back down, grabbing her white blanket, and closed her eyes. She would be back asleep before I even hit the hallway.

Luther was cleaning up the shattered chair in the dining room when I walked back into the main room. "You're an ass Luther. I hope you know that." I walked past him and headed to the little kitchen attached to the main sitting area to get Lily her tea. But before I could even start the water, a strong loud knock came from the front door.

Luther and I both stared at each other. We knew who was on the other side of that door.

CHAPTER 8
LUTHER

Virgil just glanced at me. We may have just fought, and I may want to kill him, but we both knew that one of us had to answer that door. The person on the other side was not a patient man. I got up and brushed the dirt off myself and walked to the door, steadying my breath. Damn, my ribs are gonna be messed up by tomorrow. I reached for the doorknob and pulled it open.

Before me stood our General, Vikrum Rothsberg, a giant of a man. He stood at least a few inches taller than me and Virgil, and we were both over six feet tall. He kept his blue and silver hair in a short, cropped cut close to his head on the sides, with it being slightly longer on top. His silver armor was polished like a mirror and his royal blue cape blew in the wind that I swear followed him wherever he went.

"Good afternoon, General Rothsberg. What can I do for you?" I stepped back, allowing the captain in, forgetting all about the smashed chair across the room. He studied the small seating area, the kitchen and attached dining room, the shattered debris of the chair. He glanced at Virgil behind the counter, then at me.

"Good, you and Crawley are both here. Saves me a trip. How is your father? Is he available for a meeting before we begin?" He peered at me for the answer, but I didn't have one. Virgil stepped forward.

"No sir, General Cromwell hasn't awoken for more than a few brief hours over the last few days. Captain Cromwell just returned from a hunting trip with his sister Luna moments ago." He gave a quick bow to the General. I hated it when we had to use official titles, but the General was a stickler for formalities.

"Ah, thank you Captain Crawley. I was unaware that you would know more than his own son." The General looked at me and I could feel the daggers he shot at me.

"I apologize, General. My youngest sister has had the graying for a decade now and since my father is sick with it as well, my sister Luna and I are the sole providers for the family. We were away hunting for food to feed our family. Captain Crawley and the Nightfall sisters help us take care of our family while we are away gathering supplies and hunting." I shouldn't have to explain myself to him, but without an excuse, I could lose my station.

"It is what it is. I am sorry for your sister and father's failing health. The graying isn't a curable disease. You're fortunate your sister is still alive." He spoke as he looked at the plush, worn red couch and chairs that decorated our living room.

"Would you like to have a seat? I can try to wake up my father for you?" I gestured to the living room and waited for a response before just walking out of the room.

"If you would be so kind to at least let him know I am here, I would appreciate it. Captain Crawley, when you're done with your tea, could you please come have a seat?" He glared at Virgil, but he took the seat in my father's old chair.

"I just have to take this tea to Lilly, and I will be right with you, General." Virgil bowed and took the steaming up into my sister's room. I didn't even realize he had made the damn tea. Did he learn how to make it like Luna? Did she teach him? I tried to ignore the thoughts swirling in my head as I headed towards my father's room in the back of the house. I knocked twice on the door before letting myself in.

"Boy, if you are trying to tell me again that I need to leave this room," he started coughing roughly between words, "I'll beat you with that stupid cane my dense daughter gave me. Make it good for something."

"Good to see you are awake and have your fighting spirit father," I crossed the room and opened the curtain. I could've sworn the old man just hissed at me as the light from outside filtered in through the window. The room seemed smaller than I remembered. A white sheet covered the queen-size bed, and his favorite faded green blanket covered his slowly fading body. The muscular, clean-shaven man that I remembered was slowly losing mass. He had a slightly long grey beard, his grey eyes as lifeless as Lilly's. It was maddening to watch my family break in front of me. "General Rothsberg is here and would like an audience with you if you're up to it." I stated as cooly as I could to him.

"I'm glad to see your home. Is Luna with you?" I reached for me to help him sit up. I just shook my head, apparently answer enough for him. "Well, one less person to fuss at me. When did the General arrive, did he say what he wanted?" I shook my head again.

"He just got here, he's uh, sitting in your chair in the living room." My father's eyes flashed with anger. No one sat in that chair anymore, not even him. It's been empty for ten years.

"Well then, he better move when I get out there." My father steadied himself on his weakened legs and started walking towards the door, his limp more predominant now than before. I left the door open, so it was easier to get out of the room.

"Let me help you get to the sitting room." I reached my arm out just for him to slap it away. Stubborn old man. I walked close behind him, just in case I need to catch him if he fell.

As we entered back into the sitting room, my father noticed the shattered chair across the floor. "We will talk about that when we are alone." He was pissed but wouldn't let it show with others in the house. Virgil and the General stood as my father and I entered the room. In a way of respect from the captain, but from Virgil, it was to give up his seat and to be a steadying hand if needed.

"Good afternoon, Vikrum. Please, may I ask you to move to the chair Virgil vacated? That chair is my wife's chair. No one sits in it anymore." He sat down on the couch and the General looked at me and took his seat in the chair next to Virgil. His face ghost white. It wasn't like that when he took tea to Lilly. The general gestured for me to sit next to my father. I did.

"I wish I could say it was a good afternoon Gunther, but you know as well as I do that if I am coming around, I bring no good news." The General had a grim expression on his face. The informality between my father and him showed just how much of friends there were.

"Well, get on with it, Vikrum. I have little time left and I am a tired man." I tried not to wince at his words.

"I need your services, Gunther. More so, I need Nox. He refuses to listen to anyone but you. I was hoping you might convince the dragon that someone else could command him. Maybe your son." Holy shit. He just asked my father for his best friend. His dragon, his beloved. Sometimes I thought the dragon was more family than me. My father just yawned, as if we bore him with the conversation.

"Then why not have him come see me? It's not like he can't shift and walk his ass here. Why not just ask him?" The shock on General

Rothsberg's face was real. Just like the expressions on Virgil's and mine.

"He...he can shift into a human?" that was all the general had sputtered out before the door opened and a young man about in his thirties waltz right on in without invitation. His purple hair was just like how my father used to keep his, shorter on the sides and longer on the top styled back, his sapphire eyes felt like a fire burning straight into my soul. He walked right up to my father and looked down at him. I went to move until my father rested a hand on my knee.

"Good to see you Nox," my father smiled up at the man in black. Nox clasped my father on both shoulders and lowered himself to meet my father's gaze.

"You're not supposed to be sick, my friend." His voice was like an ethereal chorus, beautiful and haunting. I wasn't sure if I should've been afraid or not.

CHAPTER 9
NOX

The man before me was no longer the strong, brave knight I knew. No, he wreaked of death and decay. The smell of a rotted apple would be a much more pleasant scent. He was, in fact, dying; I had heard him correctly before entering. My friend was living on borrowed time.

"Well, I'm not immortal now, am I?" Gunther smiled at me and rested his hand on mine. It took a lot of will not to shudder under his icy touch. He was fading faster than he was letting on. This will not be easy.

"No, I suppose you are not. I know what the General wants. If you want me to fight alongside your son, I will. I will do what needs to be done to make sure he returns home safe." His hand squeezed my knee. He knew this was just as hard for me as it was for him.

"It would honor me greatly if you took care of my son. Keep him safe for me." Gunther squeezed my knee once more before sitting back. Acceptance settled into him. Fear crept into my heart as if this would be the last time I saw my friend.

"As you wish," I turned to his son, "My name is Nox. Your father raised me as a hatchling and has taken good care of me over the years. I shall grant you my strength and my power. I ask for my freedom in return when this war is over." His eyes settled on mine, and he nodded.

"It's a deal then." He reached his hand out, and I took it, shaking it firmly one time. I heard footsteps on the stones out front, my eyes shooting to the door as the smell of vanilla, citrus and something ethereal hit my nose as the door opened.

A beautiful creature walked into the room, but tension also filled the air behind my head. Her long blue, blonde hair waved over her shoulders, her dark brown eyes looked over at us all, and my heart stopped. Who was she? And why did she smell like that? I raised up to my feet and noticed that the short-haired blonde male was on his feet and by her side taking the bags she carried into the house. Her eyes fell on me, and she smiled. Oh, I really needed to know if she was who I think she was.

CHAPTER 10
LUNA

Who in the hell is that?! The tall violet haired man stood as I entered the house. I didn't know I was interrupting a meeting. Great, more things for me to fight about when we all were alone.

I smiled at Virgil as he grabbed the bags from my hands and leaned down to whisper into my ear, "We need to talk as soon as possible." I looked past him to my father, Luther, and the General of the Royal Army.

"Ok," I whispered back. I smiled at the general and at my father. Luther could go to hell. "Good after noon General Rothsberg, I see my brother's lack of manners are still astounding. May I offer you tea or coffee?"

"Thank you Luna, if you're making some I would love a cup. A splash of milk and 2 sugars if you have it to spare. Also, you're not in rank. You can call me Vikrum you know." He was always polite to me.

"Of course, Vikrum. And you sir?" I looked at the sapphire eyed man more closely now. His hair was a deep purple, short almost to the skin on the side with a longer length on top, slicked back with what looked like some type of gel. His sapphire blue eyes held onto mine a little too long for Virgil's liking. He tapped my shoulder and held up the bags. I pointed to the counter, still waiting for a reply.

"I'm Nox, and sure, I'll take a glass of water, please." Nox, why did his name sound familiar? He was handsome, to say the least. No comparison to Virgil, but still handsome. I made my way to the kitchen and plugged in the coffeepot and placed a paper filter into the machine along with the grounds and water.

"Father, would you care for something to drink?" I asked over my shoulder. He would probably say no or nothing or some other derogatory remark. The man could be very cruel to me sometimes.

"Yes please. I don't care what it is. Surprise me." He spoke quietly, as if he was in a room far into the house. Alright, brandy with tea and honey, it was.

"Luna, I will take a glass of water too." Luther snapped his fingers at me, and I swear Nox's hand clenched into a fist. Virgil growled under his breath. I tapped his foot to get him to stop.

"You have two legs and know where everything is. Get it yourself." I shot back at him. I wasn't his damn maid. Nox and Vikrum choked on what I'm sure was a laugh or just denial that I spoke to him that way. "Ignore me gentlemen, I will bring your drinks to you shortly. Please continue as if I am not here." I went back to making their drinks, nudging the overprotective male from my side out of the kitchen. Something was wrong with him. Virgil's face was much paler than it was when I left, but I noticed the red mark on his jaw and the cuts on my brother's face. They had fought.

"Thank you Luna. Gunther, I never come bearing good news. War is breaking out near Hildaria in the South. His highness wants his dragon riders and beast riders on the front lines." I almost dropped the cups in my hands. Nox was there in a blink of an eye, grabbing the General's coffee and my father's tea from me. I nodded my thanks as he handed each of the men their cups. He followed me back into the kitchen. The men speaking in the living room continued like I didn't almost just drop everything in my hands. I peered over at Virgil, who giving me a knowing sad look. He would leave soon. And I would be stuck here alone again.

"Are you alright Luna?" Nox's voice pierced through my train of thought. I hadn't realized he was standing in front of me in the kitchen, blocking my view of the living room. "Uh, yeah. Thank you for helping me back there. I don't know what came over me." I tried not to let my hands shake as I filled his glass with water. "Here you go. Sorry, all we have for water is tap."

"It's fine. I'll go take this to sir snaps-a-lot." he huffed a laugh and took the glass over to Luther and came back to me. He grabbed the second glass off the counter and began filling it. "Would you like to go get some fresh air?" I nodded and followed him out the front door. Virgil was watching every step Nox made. My father and brother were also watching my every move. Nox closed the door behind him, and we walked over to the little patio set we had off to the side of the house and sat down. "Are you okay?"

"No, not really. But I have to be, I guess. My brother and his friend are being sent back off to war and I have two sick family members that I need to take care of. It's the usual mess around here." I looked up at him. "Your name. I've heard it before. I just don't remember where."

He smiled at me. "Well Gunther helped raise me as a hatchling along with Lilliana. I was around before Luther was born." I stared at him; mouth dropped open. He was my father's beloved dragon?!

"Wait, a minute. Hold up, you're that Nox?!" Disbelief must've filled my face because he laughed, tilting his head up to the sky.

"Yes, I am that Nox. The look on people's faces when they find out the enormous scary dragon can shift is priceless." He laughed once more and looked at me. "Luna, after this war is over, I have asked for my freedom. The General wants me to ride under the command of your brother. Your father gave me his best wishes and I plan to leave when I am done. I'm from Mirith. Your father raised me there with your mother. I plan on returning home."

My eyes shot to his, "What are you saying?" Could he know where my mind has wandered each time I think of mom?

"I'm saying I think I could use some company who might need to find some answers." His smile was a broad, devilish smile. He knew what my suspicions were about my mother.

"Are you saying she might be there? Luther told me I was stupid for thinking that. My father believes mom left us for a Fae there. Neither of them bothered to go looking for her, though." I looked at the dark green paint chipping off the iron table in front of me. He was asking me to leave with him. "Can I ask why you're telling me this?"

"Your scent, for one. Something tells me there are more than a few answers for you in Mirith. But most of all because the scent of death clings to this house. And something tells me only more death will clog this house if you stay here. Is Luther always like that with you?" Nox stared a hole into me as if reading the yes there. I nodded my head.

"It's not always like that, but him and my father both treat me like a live-in maid. I'm used to it." I shrugged my shoulders. His eyes flickered back to the door as if he heard something I could not. "Is something wrong?" I asked him.

"What about you and Captain Virgil? He seems to be your protector. Currently he's pacing about inside the door as if I'm going to kidnap you from out here and he'll never see you again." He chuckled.

I looked him in the eyes; the truth written on my face. "He was my first. I don't know if it's love or infatuation since he was my first, but we wanted to be together. Luther and my father would never allow it, and we both know it. So, we keep close but not too close to raise suspicions. We did anything. I would go to the ends of the earth for him if it meant he would be safe."

"Whose life do you value more?" A shocking question, but one he clearly wanted an answer to and one I wasn't sure I wanted to answer.

"His." I glanced down as if I just spoke shameful words to Vanalli herself. But I meant it. Virgil has been my savior for years, standing ground against both my brother and my father. I will always value the life he sees in me, even when I do not.

"Well then Luna Cromwell; I, Nox Embros; swear to you to keep safe guidance of Captain Virgil Crawley while I am close to him during this war. He will not fall as long as I can save him." His words danced around me and settled in me like a promise bond the Fae make to their own.

"Why would you promise that to me? You don't know me, and I don't know why you want to help me. Not that I'm not grateful." He smiled at my questions and shrugged his shoulders before standing.

"We're about to have company, Luna. You be safe tonight. I hope to see you again soon." He winked at me as the door opened to Vikrum, walking out with Luther and Virgil in tow. Vikrum and Virgil stopped and looked at Nox and me. Nox bowed at me with a wink and a smile, then called over to the General, "I thought your conversation was better held without tainting the ears of Gunther's daughter. She doesn't need to know the gruesome details you all were discussing. Until next time Luna." He smiled and waved a hand lazily above his shoulder as he walked over to the group.

If only he knew I was leaving tonight, and I wouldn't be back anytime soon.

CHAPTER II
LUNA

I walked back into the house, Luther, Virgil, Nox and Vikrum headed towards the local barracks to talk more. Virgil looked at me once more before leaving. I hope Nox keeps his promise. Hopefully, I would be home before he left for this horrible war. My father was still sitting on the couch when I entered the house.

"How are you feeling?" I asked as I took off my boots. He looked up at me with glassy eyes, as if he had been crying. Something told me I wasn't supposed to see him like this.

"I'm tired Luna. Come and sit with me. I need to talk to you about something." he patted the seat next to him. This was the first time in the last few years he has asked me to sit with him. It's always been Luther or Lilly that got all his praise and attention. I moved closer to the couch and sat beside him. "I'm sorry I have been harsh on you since your mother left. I have misplaced my anger on you, and that is not fair. You look so much like your mother that it hurts me. I heard the fight between you and Luther." Shame filled his eyes and mine. "You're not wrong. I stopped being a father when your mother left and left you to raise your siblings. Luther and you both should've been able to be kids, and I should've been the parent and I wasn't. I'm sorry."

My hands were shaking. What in the world was going on? Did Nox hear something I didn't? "I don't understand."

"I don't have much time. The older you are when the graying catches you, the less time you have to find a cure. When your mother left, I didn't believe that she was going to get help. She wanted to go to Lord Drake, who, as you know, she used to work for in Mirith. I wanted to believe that she just left us because I was unable, no, unwilling, to accept the help of the Fae and their healers. Your mother, on the other hand, knew they could help."

"Then why not ask those at Mistveil? They're so much closer than Mirith?" I interrupted.

"Because those at Mistveil were told by King Harold himself not to aid in the matters of the graying out of fear that a mortal illness would taint those of fae blood. However, I heard recently from Harper and Virgil chattering about when they think I'm asleep that King Harold's boys don't see it the same as he does and want to change things." He looked at me with far-off eyes. "I'm not stupid to know that you don't belong here and you only stay for the sake of Lilly. I'm also not stupid enough to know that the bags Virgil grabbed from you earlier are supplies for you to take when you try to go get help."

"I-I-You're right." I put my head down and let the tears flow freely from my eyes. "I will leave after giving Lilly her medicine tonight."

"Don't worry about it. Lilly hasn't been taking it, anyway. She has been refusing it for days. I have to give it to Kira, though. She can spike a cup of tea like a lethal assassin that one. Kira is probably the only one to deceive even me into taking my blasted medicine. But Luna, it's not working. So get help from the Fae at Mistveil. Get her the help she needs." He looked me in the eye and the pleading in them almost broke me.

"What about you? What if I can't make it back in time to save you too?" tears filled my eyes. Even though he wasn't the nicest, I didn't want to lose him either.

"I already talked to Kira and Harper. They will come to check on us while you're away. I already told them what I planned on asking you to do well before you left." He planned all of this and neither of my friends told me. I was supposed to go to their show tomorrow night. Screw it, saving my sister is way more important. They'd understand.

"Fine. I'll go pack my things." I kissed my father on the cheek and went to my room to pack my bag. I grabbed out my big green sack bag and started shoving clothes into it, a smaller tent, and a few toiletries. I hope to gods I'm back before they leave. Mistveil was about a four-day hike into the mountains. I can do this.

I walked about out of my room and opened the door across from mine to check on Lilly. She was still breathing. I stepped inside and kissed her on the forehead. "I love you. I will be back with medicine to get you better. I promise." I slipped out of her room, silently closing the door behind me. Heading back down the hall to the sitting room, I found my father still sitting on the couch. "Do you want to stay there, or would you like me to help you back to your room?" I asked as I reached the kitchen and checked the bags Virgil had left on the counter.

"I'll be fine here. Someone is going to see the boys when they get back. I'll tell them what I sent you to do. Do not look back and be careful at night. Fae are tricksters who will and can-do harm to you without touching you." My father looked once more at me; his grey eyes still rimmed with tears. I grabbed my bags and headed to the door.

"You weren't always bad, and I forgive you and I love you." I felt that this was my goodbye. That when I returned, my father would not be here to greet me. I opened the door and rushed out of it without a look back. I threw my bags into the side cart of my bicycle and set off down the cobblestone streets towards the main gate back to Wardveil.

VIRGIL

I wanted to tell her I loved her; I wanted to ask her to marry me. It would have to wait now. I fiddled with the ring box in my jacket. I should've done it right then and there. Gunther gave me his permission over a year ago, but I got called away before I could. And now, well, I was being called away again. This time was going to be much longer, more than a year. That's it. After this meeting, I'm running back there to ask her to marry me. I needed to tell her it's her and always has been her. I would burn the world for her and mark each name into the earth itself as long as she was safe. I wish I knew why Nox took her outside. I picked up my pace to match steps with Nox.

"Mind if I ask you something?"

"I didn't ask her out if that's what you want to know," Nox said flatly at me, not even looking in my direction.

"I wasn't going to ask that. Honestly, I wanted to know what you were planning on telling Luther about your chat with his sister." I genuinely wanted to know because Luther was fuming, and I knew things were going to get back. Luna was a touchy subject for him, and I don't understand why he's so obsessed with being possessive of her.

"It's none of his business what she and I discussed. It's between her and I. Same goes with you." He stopped and looked me in the eye. "Just know I have a promise I have to keep." He walked off before I could even ask what that meant. Luther, however, was following quickly behind the dragon. General Rothsberg was talking to another commanding officer, so I followed behind them just to make sure nothing was going to happen.

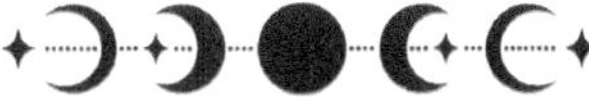

LUTHER

What the hell did this asshole think he was doing talking to my sister in private? I reached up behind Nox and shoved him into the stone wall of the barrack alleyway. "My sister is off limits to you. Do you understand me?"

"Did you just shove me?" he laughed at me. I flipped the snap off of my sheath. He would learn that I don't play games when it comes to my sisters' safety. "You might want to rethink your next move." Nox enjoyed hearing himself talk.

"Or what, you'll tell my father I wasn't nice to you? Or tell the General I threatened you?" I pulled my knife out and held it up to his throat in a warning to get him to back off.

"Oh no, not at all. Neither of them will care what I do to you. Hell, Luna herself wouldn't care what I did to you. I made her a promise and I will keep it, even if it means eliminating you in the process." His eyes started glowing a bright blue. He wouldn't change here. That would kill so many people.

"Luna is my sister. Stay the hell away from her!" I yelled into his face, and he just smiled and laughed a deeper laugh that didn't match his voice. He leaned forward, pressing my blade to his throat, and whispered. "She is my sister, too."

Before I could register his words, hands gripped me and flung me around my knife, imbedding into the flesh of my assailant. Red flowed into my hands, and I finally saw the face before me. Virgil's face twisted in pain as he reached for the blade now deep in his chest. A loud roar came from behind me. A flash of purple and blue shot past me and straight to Virgil, gripping him up and rushing him away.

Looking down at Virgil's blood on my hands, the only thought in my head was, *I killed my brother.*

CHAPTER 12
LUNA

The guards at the gate didn't stop me to ask questions about where I was going. I guess they got used to seeing me do this often enough. It was late in the evening, the pinkish blue sky ahead glittered alive with the stars in the heavens. It was a beautiful sight to behold. The forest seemed to glow this evening with the fireflies lighting up the bushes and trees, like it was lighting the way for me. The sapphire blooms were coming into view ahead, where the path forked left and right. I had to go left to head towards Mistveil. I reached the fork and began turning left when I had to slam my feet into the dirt to stop from running someone over.

"I'm so sorry I wasn't expecting—" I looked at the male in front of me closely, the shaggy orange hair, the emerald green eyes, and a jawline that looked like it could cut glass. "Oh, hi Fennik." I smiled at him.

"Good evening Luna. Did you forget we were meeting?" He asked me, looking confused.

"Yeah, I'm sorry. A lot went down when I got home." I didn't feel like explaining everything to him. There was too much going on for my head to be thinking straight.

"I hope everything is alright. I spoke with the healers at home, and they are slightly worried about helping humans, thanks to my father's scare tactics. I just didn't want you thinking I forgot about you." He said with his hands in his pockets. I know Mistveil is his home, but I don't want to ask him to help me get to the healers in the south side of the city. I can make it there on my own.

"Thank you, I appreciate it." I looked down at my bike. "My brother and I got into a fight, so I'm heading to the small cottage we used to stay in when I was a kid." A small lie, but it would keep him from staying with me longer than necessary.

"Would you like some company? At least for the journey there." I couldn't tell if his offer was genuine or if it came from concern for my safety. I shrugged my shoulders.

"Sure, it's about half a day's travel from here. At least it seems like the path is lit up for us. Are you okay if I still ride my bike? I've done enough walking today." He nodded at me, and we slowly started our trip. I should ask him about his home. I don't know much about Mistveil except what the healer's home looked like, the outside of the castle and the very limited information about the inhabitants courtesy of my schooling. Here goes nothing, "Fennik, what is your home like? Is it anything like Celvenia?"

He chuckled a little. "Honestly, I wouldn't know. My father made sure that we couldn't enter the human cities except for special occasions associated with our courts. And even with that said, it was very limited time inside. Mostly the festivities kept us in the Sanctuaries. Sheltered and safe, is what he would always say. Humans didn't like us or trust us, and he wanted to make sure that his precious princes would come to no harm. My brothers and I never liked the idea of being put in a stone cage and put on display for all to see." He looked at me with understanding. Truly, he knew what it was like to do for others, despite wanting more. He continued, "So I wouldn't be able to compare the cities well but, those in Mistveil miss the time where they and humans could live as one instead of one using the other for wants and desires. The High Priestess is one of the eldest healers we have in Mistveil. She originally asked my father years ago when the graying first became an issue, if he would build a healer's home outside the city's gates so that healers could help those inflicted with the disease. Of course, he refused for fear that his mates and children would succumb to the illness ourselves, despite her telling him it wouldn't affect us like it did your people."

"Oh, I didn't know that. Heck, I don't think any human knows a Fae wanted to help us." I interrupted. But it was true, we did not know, not a single one of my friends or family knew. Or if they did, no one ever spoke about it. I wonder if the Royal guards knew about this.

"It's not surprising. My father kept it quiet. Only those in the meeting had knowledge of the High Priestess' building plans. She had a nice design and layout from what we could see. Whoever she had design the blueprints did a fantastic job." He looked very impressed, but then it hit me. The first case of the graying in humans began over a hundred years ago.

"How old are you, Fennik?" I was looking straight ahead at the dirt path. Some roots were popping up out of the ground and I needed to pay more attention to not falling off my bike that looking at him.

"I'm six hundred and twenty-one." He spoke it so nonchalantly that it made me wobble a bit on my seat. Over six hundred years old, well, if I didn't feel young before, I felt like a child now. "I look pretty good for being an old man, huh?"

I about choked on air at his attempt to joke. "I mean, yeah, I definitely wouldn't have thought you were that old. I thought you were in your thirties or something." He laughed, and I looked over at him. He was smiling and had this look of contentment. I wonder if he spoke this freely back in his castle.

"I should probably answer your question now." he pushed back a long branch back so I could pass him. "Mistveil is more advanced than the human cities. We have vehicles that move on energy, not gas, phones that we carry in our pockets, not that stay on walls in homes. We can look up anything we want from the palm of our hands. Our cities were mostly they started like the human ones. They have skyscrapers in all sizes, buildings that look like huge water towers but their homes in the skies. The only true show of the old way in Mistveil are the Healers Temple and my family home, Castle Mistveil." He spoke so fondly of his home. I really wanted to see it. Maybe after I saw the healers, maybe I could find him and ask for a tour.

"The cabin is just up ahead." I pointed towards the small stone home, the thatched roof still intact despite years of neglect. As we got closer, I saw the red paint on the front door was fading, the fire pit was covered in grass and sticks, even the glass in the front square windows seemed to be foggy and covered in dirt and dust. I should go inside and clean up. Not like anyone besides me will visit here anytime soon.

"Would you like me to check inside to make sure the house is secure?" Fennik was at the front door, testing the doorknob. He must just assume we left it unlocked all these years. I pulled my key ring out of my jacket pocket and jingled them towards him.

"I have keys. It should still be locked." I kicked the kickstand down on my bike and left it next to the stone bench I had drawn on when I was a kid. Looking for the right key, I walked up the large stone step to get onto the patio. I found the small silver key and inserted it into the key hold and turned the knob and key together.

Fennik waited for me to move and allow him inside. He searched the bedrooms, the bathroom and the crawl space before allowing me inside. "All clear. You should be safe here. How many days will you be out here?"

"I'm unsure. Maybe a few." I wish I had kidnapped Virgil to come with me, so I wasn't alone here. "I have plans in a few days. My brother and my best friend are leaving to go to Hildaria." I walked back out of the house and headed to my bike to grab my things.

"What's going on in Hildaria?" Fennik asked from the doorway behind me. Maybe he wasn't involved in his father's plans.

"There is war beginning. Your father requested the Dragon riders and Beast riders to be on the front lines. My father was the General of the Dragon Legion. Before he had to retire, he rode his dragon Nox into battle, who will now ride with Luther and hopefully will protect my friend, too." I tried not to let the tears I have been holding back fall from my eyes.

"Luna, look at me." The demand in his eyes had me turning to face him. "There is no war going on in Hildaria. We have never had a conflict with them. We supply most of their trades and imports. My father wouldn't request war to happen so close to our home. He would just cut trades and imports." The urgency in his voice had me on alert.

"What do you mean? I heard the plans myself. Usually, the meetings happen a week before they plan to depart." Panic laced my words. Should I return home and demand answers? No, Lilly needed me to get to the healers. Luther could handle himself.

"Who gave the command to your brother?" His eyes went from a bright jade green to a dark forest green so quickly, something wasn't right.

"General Rothsberg, General of the Royal Army." I said flatly. Was the General planning a war to divide the Fae territories and using the King as a pawn? I wouldn't say the man didn't have ambitions because he definitely did. But this may be more than even I realized.

"I'm sorry to leave you, but I need to go see my father immediately." Fennik was down the step and next to mine in a blink of an eye. "Please be sure to lock the door tonight. If you see a wolf outside, do not open the door and offer it food. Just know its someone checking on you." I nodded my head even though I wanted to yell at him for the food comment. I blinked and a large orange wolf took up the space he just occupied. He took off behind the cottage and went down the path.

I went into the house with bags in hands and closed the door behind me. Clicking the lock shut.

CHAPTER 13
FENNIK

She had to be wrong. There is no way my father would start a war with Hildaria. They have been our allies for centuries. I rush up through the iron gates to the castle, the sapphire blooms lining the walkway. The moon was full and high tonight, stars blinking into existence as I made my way up to the large oak doors. The guards saluted and pulled open the heavy doors before I got within twelve feet of them. Damian and Bastian were seated at a small table in front of the fireplace in the entry hall as I shifted back into my fae form.

Damian's crimson eyes shifted towards me. His messy red hair barely pulled back moved just a bit to reveal his slightly pointed ears. "What's wrong Fennik? You look like you've seen a ghost." He mused while pushing an ivory marble piece across the board. I never learned how to play chess; it seemed boring to me.

"Have either of you talked to Father lately?" I asked them between panting breaths. Bastian looked at me and took in my expression.

"No, what's got you so out of breath? You're usually more put together, like a little schoolboy heading to class. One of your case studies catch you?" Bastian was a right prick. He made a quick move with an ebony chess piece.

"Would you happen to know anything about a war breaking out in Hildaria?" I asked both of my brothers. Finally able to catch my breath, I plopped down on the red velvet chair between them. Their heads shot up to meet my gaze. By the wide eyes and Bastians gapping mouth, I'd be correct in assuming that's a no.

"Where did you hear this shit?" Bastian spit out at me.

"Celvenia, apparently General Rothsberg is saying that our father is about to go to war with Hildaria. Putting the dragon and beast riders at the front lines. I don't know about you two, but I wouldn't think father would do that." I stared past my brothers at the fire in the stone fireplace, losing myself in the swirls of reds, yellows and oranges. I settled deeper into the chair. "Damian, that girl from Wardveil, she's in a cottage close to here. She's the one who told me. Her brother is Captain Luther Cromwell, and her father is General Gunther Cromwell, former commander of the dragon legion. She comes from a family whose served ours well over the last few decades. Can you check on her later? I want to go to the villa and see if I can get an audience with our father. Hell, I'll even take speaking with my mother if I can't talk to him."

Damian nodded his head. "Sure thing. Maybe see if Nik or Val know anything about this. But as the beast's commander, I know nothing of a request coming through for troops." He looked over at Bastian, who was toying with what looked like a pawn. "What about you? Any chatter with your legion of bats?"

"Not a word. Everything has been quiet. Are we sure her intel is right?" He set the piece back on the board and looked at me. "Can she be trusted?"

"Her brother is going off into the war with the Dragon riders. I highly doubt she would've made it up." I get where he was coming from, but I trusted my gut with this one. I looked at Damian. He nodded and stood.

"I'll go check on the cottage. Shouldn't take too long. I'll report back shortly. Bastian, why don't you help him with Val and Nik? They probably won't help if you don't threaten them." Damian turned and headed for the door, waving a hand over his head.

"You really need a backbone against those two kid. But since Damian thinks you'll need my help, let's go see the assholes." Bastian stood up and grabbed my arm to follow him towards the grand staircase in the middle of the room. "Is she hot?" he asked.

The question made my head snap towards him. "Why in the hell would you ask me that?" I choked out at him.

"Well, you're concerned for her safety, and you never care for any of the women around here. So, is she hot or not?" He smirked at me, and I wanted to punch him.

"I'm not responding to that. The women around here fawn over you, Nik and Val. I'm completely fine with not showing them any unnecessary attention." I continued up the marble stairs, the blue carpet covering the center of the stairs was slightly worn from where we all ran up and down the stairs for decades. I'm honestly surprised it still has any cushion to it at all.

Bastian shrugged his shoulder and made a right at the top of the stairs heading to the summer wing, Valyns' part of the castle. Gods, it's about to get really sticky.

CHAPTER 14
DAMIAN

The night air was refreshing. Cool but not freezing, the stars and moon in the sky sung together like an icy rush across my skin. This was my favorite type of evening, the crickets chirping in the distance; the frogs croaking a song to one another for company. I should shift and run there, but this was a rare evening. Quiet and peaceful, no bickering brothers driving me insane, no needing to chase after Fennik to make sure the idiot wasn't getting hunted. I rolled my eyes at my last thought. Only he would find someone who tried to kill him alluring.

The wind picked up a little, breathing through my grey cotton shirt and jean. If the wind was going to be mean to me now, it was time to shift to keep myself warm. Clearing my mind of any thoughts besides picturing my large black wolf, my limbs elongated, bones breaking, cracking and healing back in place. The worst part of this was the pain of my face elongating. My senses completed the shift, my eyes adjusting to the sharper sight. The scents of the blood lilies and the sapphire blooms filled my nose with the sweet smell of roses and honey. I picked up on Fenniks faint scent of firewood and autumn air; it was coming from directly down the path into Wardveil. I wonder if the humans realized how easy it was for us to reach them from here. The people of Mistveil kept to their city beyond the castle. A left at the end of this path would take me right to the city and normally I would head there with Bastian by now, but I sadly have a different duty this evening. Oh, Fennik was going to owe me big time for skipping out on seeing the lovely Rita tonight.

I banked a right at the end of the path and headed into Wardveil to go pay a visit to his mystery woman.

LUNA

I am not staying here long. Fennik should be long gone by now, and I had to head to Mistveil before dawn. Hopefully, whoever he sent out to monitor me wouldn't be here for a while. I pulled all my stuff from my bag and heard a soft clink of metal on the wooden floor. I looked down and saw a small silver locket on a chain right beneath the edge of the bed. I reached down to pick it up, turning it over in my hand. A light silver locket with a painted sapphire bloom on the front and my initials on the back. This is not mine. How did it get in the bag? I noticed a piece of paper tucked in the pocket of the jean jacket I pulled out of the bag; I pulled it out and read it...

Dear Luna,

I honestly don't know how to say this, but I have to get this off my chest. I am no good at expressing my feelings and even though we agreed to keep what we have between us; I don't want to anymore. I want the world to know that I love you and want to call you mine. I get your worry with Luther but screw him. It's your life and you deserve to live it the way you want to. So, what do you say? Be mine?

Love,

Your Pain in the Ass,

Virgil

P.S.: Open the locket. I think you'll like it.

I clutched the note to my chest, tears streaming down my cheeks. I wish I would've seen this before I left. A thousand times over, it would be a yes. I folded up the letter and put in back in the pocket. I clicked open the locket to find a small picture on one side. It was the last picture we took together at the midsummer festival. He was holding onto me while Kira snapped the picture. The other side of the locket just had our initials in a heart. I closed the locket and put it on. When I get back home, he will be mine. More of a reason to hurry the hell up and not wait here. I quickly changed into a pair of thicker tight blue jeans and my favorite black shirt, pulling on the jean jacket and my boots. It was time to go. I threw everything back in the bag, quickly made a sandwich, and started packing my bike back up.

According to my old textbooks, Mistveil was maybe an hour or so north of here. It shouldn't take me long. I went back into the house one last time to make sure I wasn't forgetting anything. Looking around, I thought to myself, maybe Virgil and I could live here when all this crap was over with. That would be very nice. I grabbed my keys from the low-lying table by the door and locked up the house behind me. Mounting my bike, I started my trek towards Mistveil.

DAMIEN

The trip to the cottage was a short one. The lights were off inside. Maybe she was asleep, and my night detail would be simple. I needed to just find what room she was in and make sure she's still alive, then report back to Fennik and then head to the city to see Rita. I wonder if Bastian is going to see her when he's done.

I walked up to the windows at the front of the little stone home; they were covered in dust. Luckily, I was tall enough in this form that I could see inside without needing to shift back. Living room, dining room; empty. Front bedroom; empty, back two rooms, both empty. This isn't a good sign. I stalked up to the back door and calmed my breathing. Listening for any sounds of life inside, I heard nothing. Where the hell was she?

Sniffing around the front door, I picked up the slightest smell of citrus and vanilla, and something else; ethereal, like an enchanted wind off the sea. Well, I didn't smell that the other night. I followed the scent to the back of the cottage, and I noticed a small path with what looked like fresh tire marks from a peddle bike. Wait, she wouldn't be out in the middle of the night going somewhere, would she? Did she not know what was out on this side of the forest at night?

I shot off down the path after her. Gods, don't let me be too late.

CHAPTER 15
LUNA

The fireflies were few and far between out here, the tree tops blocked out most of the star and moonlight. I was not expecting it to be so much denser this far back. Wardveil had its mysteries for sure. The smell of something ungodly sweet hit my nose, it wasn't a good smelling sweet either. Like bittersweet smell of rotten fruit. A deep growl came up behind me. I peddled harder to quickly get away from whatever was off in the tree line.

Leaves were rustling and crunching beneath the tires of my bike as I kept rushing down the dirt path. Limbs and stray vines whipped and grabbed at me from both sides. A thorny branch tangled in my hair as I tried to pass underneath it and it flung me back off the seat of my bike. I hit the hard dirt ground, my bike collapsing a few feet away. I heard laughter coming from the darkness all around me; I started pulling at my hair to get it free from the thorns. Footsteps thudded on the path behind me. I pulled hard on the last few strands of hair, freeing them from the thorny branch. The footsteps behind me picking up into what sounded like a running pace. I refused to look back. I scrambled for my bike and launched into a sprint and jumped onto my bike, peddling harder than before.

A sharp pain shot through the back of my head. My vision blurred, the bike wobbling beneath me. Something hit the dirt in front of me. Was that thing throwing rocks at me?! I had to keep going; I was not about to die here at the hands of some creature. I shook my head vigorously to clear my vision. Everything was still hazy, but I could make out the tree line up ahead, almost there. My front tire hit a hole in the path that I didn't see, and I collapsed. A shooting pain shot through my right leg as the creature jumped on my bike, pinning me beneath it.

The oily blackish green creature smiled at me with too white sharp teeth. It laughed in my face as it leaned down to sniff me. It had two horns on the sides of its head, one long bone white horn on the left and a broken-down black stump on the right. It wore what looked like a burlap sack as pants, no shirt to be seen, but a belt across its chest filled with knives of different shapes and sizes. My breath caught as I realized a Borg hunted me. They are notorious for hunting down humans and Fae alike and feasting on them. I thought they were only in the south of the continent, not all the way up here.

I stilled. My knife was still strapped to my right leg, but I couldn't reach down far enough to get it. The Borg lifted a rock high above its head and brought it down hard on the left side of my head. I felt the warm blood trickle down my face, my blurry vision only getting worse. The world was blackening around me. The Borg lifted its hand with the rock once more, about to drive it home on my skull until a darkness crept over me and I slipped into the black abyss.

Chapter 16
Bastian

Fennik is hiding something about this woman. I just know it. She's got to be smoking hot if she's got his attention, or maybe she's not. Who knows with him? Either way, she's not my primary concern right now. There is no way our father, arrogant as he is, would start a war with Hildaria. They are good people and great allies to us. I started thinking about all the trade routes and the supply chains. One thing I had to pay attention to thanks to dear old dad. I looked over my shoulder. Fennik was dripping sweat.

"Dude, lose the jacket. You know this wing is hot as balls, you should be used to a little heat though. Isn't your wing slightly warm as well?" I called back over my shoulder. Valyn was probably all the way in his lavish pool down the hallway.

"My wing is comfortable, comparable to Niks' wing. You guys don't seem to mind hanging out there when you're bored." Fennik shot back at me while taking his jacket off and hanging it over his arm.

"Touché. Think Lord Summer is lounging about in his pool?" I chuckled. Gods, this hallway felt never ending. The carpeting covering the floors changed a few doors back into a sea-foam green. The hardwood beneath the carpet creaked and groaned under our steps.

"Yeah, probably. You would think he lives in it." He pushed past me and stopped in front of a teal door and knocked three times. His knocks weren't as assertive as they should've been.

I walked up next to him and banged on the door before barging in. I heard some type of protest by Fennik, but I didn't care too much to hear what he was saying. The room was hot and muggy; the pool took up a majority of the room from one side to the other. But I have to say he had one of the best views. The pool opened up to a huge wall length window with a stunning view of the mountains. The chiffon white curtains were pulled back wide open. A large splash came from the far side of the pool. Not surprisingly, a large great white shark was splashing about.

"Oh, come on Valyn, we need to talk to you!" I shouted into the pool, hoping the idiot could hear me.

"What's going on that you have to interrupt me?" The large shark popped its head through the window top of the water and looked directly at us.

"Dude, it is creepy when you talk through one of you animal forms." A shiver ran down my spine. It was, in fact, creepy as shit, seeing those teeth smiling at me.

He shifted forms, but decided to forgo the clothing this time. Great, just what I wanted to see today. "What is it?"

"Do you know anything about talks of a war between us and Hildaria?" Fennik asked first, going straight for the topic at hand, no pleasantries at all. Well, this was indeed new and also concerning.

Hauling himself from the pool, Valyns silver hair looked a little darker with the water running down his face into his beard. He wiped the water from off his face. "What war?" The look of confusion on his face must have mirrored the look from mine and Damians earlier because Fennik sighed.

"According to someone I met, General Rothsberg is gathering the dragon and beast legions, saying that our father is starting a war with Hildaria and wants the legions on the front lines." Fennik's words seemed to silence even the water.

"Are you sure? As far as I know, we are on good terms with Hildaria. Why would dad even bother with war when we could just stop trading or put holds on certain supplies they need?" Valyn finally grabbed a towel and wrapped it around his waist.

"That's what we said when Fennik told us. There was no point to war when Hildaria has done nothing to bring it on." I said, still standing up against the wall.

The door kicked in a moment later, "Hello dear brothers, your god has arrived." The blonde-haired asshole has entered the room like the ass he is. Waving his hands up and down his body in a display of arrogance. I rolled my eyes.

"Niklaus, why the hell did you kick in my door?!" Valyn roared at him as Nik made his way towards the pool.

"Well, you all keep forgetting to let me in on your little meetings, so I decided I'd invite myself in." Niklaus looked at me and winked. Gods, he was high as a kite right now, but Fennik was gonna charge forward regardless of Nik's state of mind.

"Is our father starting a war with Hildaria?" Fennik was forward with him. No bullshit. When I told him he needed a backbone against these two, I wasn't expecting him to actually grow one on the walk here.

"Why on earth would he do that?" Nik had the smarts to look concerned, which for him right now said something. He grabbed at the cream-colored lounging chair and could barely sit and look Fennik in the eyes. "I haven't heard anything on that front. Why are you saying this Fenny?"

"I hate that nickname, Klaus. But I heard that the General of Celvenia is gathering the dragon and beast legions at quote father's request to the front line." He used air quotes but had a serious look on his face.

"What has Damian heard of this?" Valyn joined them, sitting out on another lounge chair in front of the pool.

I guess I should sit down too. I grabbed a chair and pulled it over to them, and sat down.

"Damian hasn't heard anything about this either, but we want to take this serious. Could you imagine if someone started a war and claimed they were doing it in the name of King Harold? It wouldn't end well." Fennik said to them. "I sent Damian to go watch over the person who gave me the information. I don't think she realized what she was telling me. But I want to go see father and since you two," he pointed between Nik and Val. "Seem to have father's ear more than any of us. Do you think you could either talk to him on my behalf or possibly get me a meeting with him?"

Val sighed. "I can make a phone call. Ulrich should be with him today. Maybe he can get us a meeting with him, but be prepared for it to take a few days. Hopefully, the mention of potential war will speed up the process." He stood and went for his phone. Before reaching it, we heard a loud roar coming from the front door and our heads snapped up.

Damian was home, and something was wrong.

CHAPTER 17
DAMIAN

I busted through the doors to the house screaming, scaring the poor housekeeper who was cleaning the living room. She took off down the hallway and I barely recognized her in my rage. "FENNIK! BASTIAN!" I yelled from the bottom of the steps. My voice rang through the halls. They would hear me wherever they were.

Bastian and Valyn were the first two I saw running down the hall, followed by what looked like a high Niklaus and an overly sweaty Fennik. They were down the steps in a few seconds.

"What's wrong?" Fennik's eyes were wide as he took in the blood on my chest. My jeans torn at the seams and knees. I knew they could smell her on me, but only Fennik would recognize it. "What happened? Where is she?!" Panic laced his words.

"She's with High Priestess Maggie in the Mor. She wasn't in the cottage when I got there, but I picked up her scent and followed her. A Borg attacked her." My brother's eyes widened. They knew the Borgs didn't live up here, and they were very far, far away from home.

"What the hell was a Borg doing in Wardveil?" Bastian was seething through his teeth. He had a nasty run in with a Borg about 30 years ago and he's had a chip on his shoulder towards them since.

"Hell, if I know, but I did what I could. I wasn't able to kill it and get her out safely. So, it's still out there." I looked at Bastian and smiled. His eyes flashed a granite hue, and Valyn knew what that meant.

He grabbed Bastian by the shoulder. "Let's go hunting, brother." Bastian smiled wickedly and nodded.

"It will be gone before morning," Bastian said, and he and Valyn took off out the front doors, shifting into their wolves halfway down the drive.

"The Priestesses told me to leave and not return until morning. I'm not about to piss them off, so we are to stay put until morning light. That should give Nik sometime to sober up." I said, looking over at Nik, who somehow managed to get himself onto the red velvet couch across from the fireplace. I'm pretty sure he was snoring, too. "Any word on if you can get a meeting with father?"

Fennik caught my line of sight and looked at Nik, "Valyn was going to call Ulrich, but then we heard you roaring and ran down here. What happened Damien?"

"I don't know. I got to the cottage, and it was empty. No lights, no sounds, nothing. I picked up her scent, heading down the dirt path behind the cottage and I followed her. I was more worried about her encountering a damn mountain lion or a bear, not a damn Borg." I shook my head and sat on the other couch. Fennik sat next to me and put his hand on my shoulder. I was still shaking, and didn't even realize it until he touched me, grounding me. "I caught the scent of the Borg before I saw or heard it. She must've heard it because she started kicking it into high gear on that bike. She got knocked off once by a thorn bush and a second time by the Borg. It got her twice with a rock and if I wasn't able to charge it when I did, that third blow probably would've killed her, Fenn. She would've died and it would've been my fault." I put my head in my hands. Something pulled me towards her, a voice whispering in my head to run faster, to be stronger. I didn't know why I had this panicking feeling, but when I saw her there laying on the ground pinned under her bike, I lost it.

"She's not dead, and that's thanks to you. So don't beat yourself up over it." Fennik patted me on the shoulder and got up. "If she's at the Mor, then she is safe. I'm going to get shower and clean off this disgusting sweat. Should we just leave Nik on the couch?" He looked over to Nik who was sprawled on the couch now. We were gonna have to fill him in on everything again in the morning.

"Leave him there. He'll wake up and either smoke more, get food or head to his room. I'm gonna go get cleaned up too. I'll go in the morning and check on her." I wasn't about to tell him I wanted to head back tonight and sit in her room until she woke up. It took the High Priestess's personal guard to remove me from the room. I should go sleep on the floor outside of the room, or at least in one of the guest rooms there. Fennik was already heading up the stairs to his wing. I got up and grabbed a blanket from the basket by the fireplace and tossed it over Nik. Not that he needed it, but I figured the staff would appreciate a covered Nik because he liked to strip in his sleep.

I walked behind the stairs to the other stairwell behind the grand staircase. I pushed open the wooden door, the sconces lit up as I closed the door behind me. The steps were blanketed with a black plush carpet; the sconces were encased in a frosted glass. These stairs led down to my domain of the castle. Being the Prince of the solar realms is a lot for one person to take on, but as the firstborn, this task was gifted to me. I have four different realms to take care of, whereas my brothers get the courtesy of helping one another out. I kind of wished I got some help with my realms, but apparently I am just superb at taking on big tasks. I sighed to myself.

My feet hit the bottom landing, a stone floor with four doors each leading to a different realm of mine, Dawn, Day, Dusk and Night, and one that lead to a room here, not a pleasant view at all. My favorite realm was the Night realm, the view of the night stars there was the best anywhere in all the realms. The city sparkled like diamonds under the full moonlight. My home there was much nicer than the small room I kept here or one of my other homes in the other realms.

I grabbed the doorknob for the night realm, a dark cherry oak door with a full moon engraved in the middle. I pushed the door open. I'm going for a swim in the lake under the stars tonight.

CHAPTER 18
LUNA

The morning light was blinding, and the smell of pancakes and maple syrup filled my nose. My eyes shuttered open, the bright light stinging my eyes. As they adjusted, I took in the room, stone and cream-colored walls on three sides of the room the wall to my left was windows from floor to ceiling with blue and gold chiffon curtains that were pulled back to show the beautiful mountain ranges in the distance, the sea of orange and red trees surrounding the mountains base. It was breathtaking if I was being honest with myself. But where in the hell was I? The last thing I remembered was being hit by the Borg and everything going black around me. How in the hell did I even survive?

I looked over at the side table and saw the plate of pancakes smothered in syrup, with a large glass of orange juice next to it. It smelled so good; I sat up and grabbed the porcelain plate and brought it onto the bed in front of me. A pewter knife and fork set nicely on the side table on a napkin. This place was beautiful and majestic, that's it. I was dead and if this was my afterlife, then so be it.

The large circular oak door with iron hinges and knob slowly creaked open. A tall beautiful, ebony slender woman entered the room, her beautiful blue pleated dress and porcelain white flats accentuated her skin. "Oh, you're awake. I'm sorry Miss. Is the food to your liking. I can get you more if you'd like." She bowed and clasped her hands in front of her.

"Oh, I haven't had a chance to eat yet. Can I ask you a question?" She nodded and let me continue. "Where am I?" "You're at the Mor, Miss. Prince Damian brought you to the high priestess last night, saying you were in a fight with a Borg and that it messed you up badly. He wasn't wrong. You came in with a fractured skull and a broken right leg. You might have a slight headache, but for the most part, the high priestess healed everything up. I'll go get the High Priestess. She can talk to you more." She bowed her head and let herself out, softly shutting the door behind her. I returned my attention to the plate of pancakes and dug in. The fluffiness of the pancake mixed with the sweetness of the syrup was heavenly. It felt like it was melting in my mouth. This was probably the best pancake I have ever had, including the ones I made back home.

The door creaked open once more and a tall red headed bearded man walked into the room, his tight green shirt hugged his muscular arms, the blue jeans he had on looked like they might bust at the seams if he squatted too far down. His crimson eyes pinned me to the bed, scanning me from head to toe. I felt completely naked under his gaze, like he could see through the white nightdress someone put me in. "Are you alright?" his voice was deep, soothing and rich.

"Uh, yeah. And you are?" I set my now empty plate back on the side table and pulled the blanket up higher towards my chest as he sat in the seat next to the bed.

"My names Damian. I'm Fennik's' older brother. When he came home last night after speaking with you, he asked me to go check in on you to make sure you were safe. But seeing as you were riding a bike through the woods and getting attacked by a Borg, I guess his suspicions of you needing to be watched were right." He looked down towards my legs and a flash of what looked like hunger flickered in his eyes. Damian looked up at me once more, his eyes the color of blood danced. My core turned molten at the way he stared into my eyes. What the hell was wrong with me?!

I closed my eyes and composed myself, "Thank you, the woman who was in here before you said that you rescued me from the Borg. I didn't realize they were up around here. I thought they only lived in the southern part of the continent." I shook my head, trying to erase the creature's face from my memory.

"They're not usually around here. Two of our other brothers went out hunting it after I brought you here. They killed it, so no worries.

It won't be tracking you down." He looked at the empty plate on the table. "Are you still hungry? We can bring more food up for you."

I shook my head, "No, I will be alright. Thank you, though." I smiled at him and grabbed for the juice, but he was quick. He grabbed the juice off the table and handed it to me. The door opened again and a familiar orange haired male walked into my room. "Hi, Fennik." I smiled weakly at him. I should've just told him the truth and maybe I would've been safer. It took me a moment to notice he wasn't alone. Behind him stood a mountain of a man. His long black hair pulled up into a man bun, his eyes the color of granite searched the room as if he was on alert for some hidden danger. His beard was wild and nowhere near as well kept as Damians. As he walked into the room, I got to see the muscles in his arms and back flex as he pulled up two chairs to the opposite side of the bed.

"Luna, you've met my eldest brother Damian, this is my other older brother Bastian." Fennik waved a hand between his brothers then to me, "This is Luna Cromwell, General Cromwell's eldest daughter."

"Hey," Bastian threw up a half assed two-finger salute with a smile. "You look like you've seen better days."

I ran my fingers through my hair and sure enough; it was a tangled mess. I touched my fingers to my temple, where the rock hit my face and winced. Oh yeah, definitely a bruise there. I didn't dare look at my leg; I know the lady said it was broken but was working on being healed. I sure as hell didn't trust my eyes currently.

"Why in all the gods' names were you out there last night Luna?" Fennik made the guilt in my stomach want to bring back up my breakfast.

"Truthfully Fennik," I looked down at my hands fiddling my thumbs together, "I was trying to come here and ask for help from the healers myself. I figured if I begged for their help, they might decide to take pity on me." I was a fool to think I could do it on my own. I heard a deep laugh from the end of the bed where Bastian was seated looking at me.

"You're either really brave or a massive idiot. My bet is half and half, but hey at least you made it here courtesy of a borg attack." This man was making a joke about what had happened to me. Honestly, I don't know if I'm more pissed or annoyed.

"Yeah, well, I wasn't expecting to be attacked by something that doesn't live around here." I spat back with venom in my words.

"Woah viper tongue, I was just saying good for you. You're here, but good luck with the begging. Most won't hear you out. They don't want to fall out of good graces with our father." Bastian said, leaning back in the chair.

"The High Priestess might hear your plea. She has a softer spot for those in need. But I cannot guarantee it. She is your personal caretaker while you're here healing up." Damian looked at me, then at his brothers. "Hope is never a thing to mock or laugh at Bastian. If it was, then we would've been screwed centuries ago."

CHAPTER 19
LUNA

I stared at the Princes in my room. I still wasn't sure if I was in a dream, a nightmare, or just dead. But these men were gorgeous and well too pleasing on the eyes. Silenced had crept across after Damian's last words about hope not being something to mock. I appreciated his stance, though.

Just then a soft knock came from the door and Bastian was up and opening it for a tall, delicate woman. Her blonde hair was glittering with silver strands and her teal eyes glistened with a golden hue around the iris. She was lovely to look at. Her pleated dress was a darker blue than the dress of the woman from earlier. The princes bowed to the woman; she must be the high priestess. She walked over to the bed and Damian stood and offered her his seat. She smiled and sat down next to me.

"Good morning, Prince Fennik gave me the impersonal introduction of who you are this morning. I am the High Priestess here at the Mor. You may address me as such or, seeing as you are not from around here, you may call me Maggie. These boys have been raised for centuries around me and still refuse to use my name over my title to my face. It can be annoying at times." She smiled at me and put a slender hand on mine. "Well, Luna, you are heal up nicely. Faster than we normally see with humans but that's not a bad thing. There was some damage done to your face and the back of your head from the attack, and you will have some bruising there over the next few days. Your leg, however, we managed to heal the break for the most part but you can't put too much pressure on it just yet. I say at least three weeks' rest and rehabilitation here will get you right back where you were before the attack. Unless you continue to fast heal. In that case, maybe 2 weeks."

Panic set in. I don't have two to three weeks. Virgil and Luther would leave by the week's end. "I don't have that kind of time. My father sent me here to beg for your help in curing my sister of the graying. My brother and best friend leave for war by week's end. I have to go back." I shook my head. I have to be there when they leave.

"I can send word to your family. As far as the matter with the graying. I will look into what I can do for your family from here. I will send one of the princes to your family home to check in on them for you. I just need more information." She pulled out a notepad from the drawer next to the bed and grabbed a pen. I started filling her in on my sister's history, the medicine the local physicians gave her. When I got to the part about my mother, she stopped writing.

"You said your mother left ten years ago to head to Lord Drake's castle. He is in Mirith, correct?" I nodded, and she made another note on her pad. "Do you know if she made it there?"

"No, we have heard nothing about her whereabouts in years. My father assumed she just left us to go live with Lord Drake. She worked for him for a very long time. My siblings and I used to go to Mirith for the summer and spend time there with them." I looked away from them and out the window towards the mountains as if I could see all the way to Mirith. I missed my mother dearly. I wondered if I would ever see her again. My eyes started to tear up, but I quickly wiped them away.

"I'll call over to the Listhrum. It's our equivalent in Mirith. The High Priestess there could tell me if she showed up there at all." Maggie looked at me with sympathy in her eyes. She must know what's going through my head and her mind must be thinking the worst. "I'll let you know when or if I get word."

She stood up and checked my pulse and muttered something to the Princes. She excused herself from my room and the princes took up their positions around my bed again.

"Lunch will be sent up shortly. She is going to write a letter to your family and I will take it shortly." Damian said as he pulled his seat closer to the bed, staring down his brothers.

"My friends Kira and Harper should be at the house as long as you're there before seven. They have a ballet tonight in the theater. I was supposed to go." I stared down at my hands. Bastian leaned in closer at the foot of the bed, drawing my eyes up to him. He put both his elbows on the edge, resting his chin on his knuckles. My eyes traveled down his arms and lingered a little too long at where I assumed his chiseled abs would be.

"I'll make sure his slow ass gets there in time, then." Bastian said to me, and his words were like liquor, smooth with a bite to them. Fennik rolled his eyes and cleared his throat. I looked at him, half forgetting he was in the room. Damian and Bastian had a gravitational pull towards them. It was unnerving.

"Luna, you're more than welcome to stay here at the Mor or we could move you into our home. Foods good, company might annoy you but at least you can be comfortable. It's completely up to you." He looked down at his hands, waiting, I realized, for my rejection. I sighed. I could stay here and lay in this bed all day, but maybe at the castle, I could get out of bed and see Mistveil.

"I'll go to your home on one condition," they all leaned forward, waiting on bated breath, "I don't want to be confined to a room or a bed all day. I want to feel free."

CHAPTER 20
NOX

I needed to hurry. Virgil was bleeding out fast. This idiot really tried to save me, me of all people. I gripped him tighter in my arms. Not fully shifting to my full size made things slightly difficult, but I could use my magic like this.

"Stay awake Virgil!" I shouted as the wind whipped at our faces. No handed magic was a pain in the ass to use, but visualizing is what I had to do. I pictured the black glittering portal that would take me home to Mirith. I pictured the ivory spiral tower of the Lithstrum, focusing on the high balcony at the top. A few feet before us a portal of darkness rippled open in the air. Thank the gods someone was looking out for me. I shot straight for the ripple and through it. The darkness started forming the shape and outline of the Lithstrum. Slowly, it started coming into clearer view, the night sky mirroring off of the Kilspur Ocean just beyond the Mitos Mountains. I saw the top balcony and flew hard for it gripping Virgil tighter to my chest. His blood was iron rich and sticky, clinging to my clothes.

They must've sensed my arrival because Bethany was on the rooftop waving at me with two others, a stretcher sitting between them. I landed and laid him on the stretcher. "He was stabbed trying to save me. His pulse is weakening, and he has lost a lot of blood. We have to save him, Beth." I looked into her emerald, green eyes, her black curly hair braided back into two plaits down her back. She nodded and started shouting at the other two in Skothi, her native tongue.

They took off towards the stone ramps down into the tower below. I followed behind them, not that I didn't trust them. I promised Luna nothing would happen to him, and I already messed up. He has to make it.

Bethany and the other two hit the bottom landing and took off down a long stone hallway, assorted plants potted in ceramic pots lines the hallway, windows filtered in the moonlight, the sconces on the walls were dim compared to the full moon's glow. They turned into a room and Beth pointed at a canary yellow chair outside the room. I assume that means I have to sit here and wait. I sat in the chair and tried not to let my mind wander to the worst-case scenario. Luther is going to pay for this. It's his fault that Virgil is now bleeding out all over the bed in there. I could smell his blood through the door, and the pungent odor of whatever medicine Beth was using smell rancid.

There was screaming and grunting down the hall. I guess he wasn't the only one being worked on tonight. I wanted to pace the hall; I wanted to punch the stone wall in front of me. It wouldn't do anything to make this time pass any faster and would just either break my hand or break the stone. I need them to hurry. Give me something to calm these thoughts. The door opened and out came one of the two men who was on the roof. He wasn't tall, his messy brown hair was dripping with sweat. The round man looked at me with sympathy in his eyes.

"She will be out soon to speak with you, sir." he bowed to me and walked off down the hall and into another room. He must be on call for help tonight.

From behind the door, I could hear whispers. I recognized Beth's voice immediately. She had a sweet, calming tone to her; I guess that's what made her so good at her job. The other female voice was low and delicate, one I didn't know, and I couldn't place the accent either. She sounded like she was speaking Skothi, but her accent was much thicker than Beths. The door opened again and this time I stood waiting patiently. Beth and the woman exited the room. Beth nodded at the girl who walked off down the hallway and into the same room as the short, round man.

"He's barely alive, Nox. What the hell happened to him?" She looked at me with prying eyes and I knew I had to tell her what happened, and so I did. Her eyes widened as I recounted the details for her. Only when I stopped talking did she breathe and sighed, "Well, his wound is deep. It's going to take a while for it to heal, but that is going to leave one hell of a scar across his chest. At minimum, he needs to stay in this room and in this bed for a few weeks."

"He's part of the Royal Army, Bethany. He's not going to sit in a bed while there are things he has to do back home." I didn't want to alert her to what was being planned. I don't believe the King would send an army here, but with me on the front lines, I could stop a lot of bloodshed. Hopefully, the General was wrong when he said Hildaria, and he meant somewhere else. If not, things just got very complicated.

"Well then, good thing you're here then now, isn't it Nox." She said my name as if it was a period in her sentence. She was giving me an order and one that I had to obey. No one disrespected a healer here or in Mistveil. That was one good way to make sure they would not help you in the future. I've seen those disrespect them before and they weren't allowed back into Lithstrum again. They had to go to the local physicians, who were usually rejected from Lithstrum due to lack of magical abilities.

"Guess I should head home then and get my things and move in here," I said like the smartass I was, bowing to her.

"Just go home and come back in the morning. He needs rest and lots of it. I'm sure he will be happy and grateful for you bringing him here to us." I smiled at her and went to give her a hug, half expecting her to shove me away, but she just embraced me back. She pulled back and looked down at her red pleated dress. "Well, it's a good thing we wear red here. Go home and get cleaned up. We got this taken care of here." She turned away from me and headed down the hallway to another room, still making her rounds.

I looked at the door one last time before walking away, back towards the roof. It was time to head home.

CHAPTER 21
LUNA

Fennik left about an hour ago to get me a room set up at their home. I have no idea what to expect, but Bastian and Damian seem to think I need guarding and have been pacing in front of the door since he left. But something clicked. "I have no clothes here. Would you happen to have grabbed my bag and my bike?" I asked, looking at Damian.

"Your bike is being looked at by one of the city's mechanics and as far as your clothes, one of the maids at the house is currently washing what was in your bag. Between blood and dirt, things got messy." He looked apologetic, like it was his fault, but he wasn't the one who caused me to bleed. I reached up to my neck and felt bare skin and panicked.

"I had a necklace on. Please tell me you have it!" I started hyperventilating. I couldn't have lost it. Bastian walked over to the side table and opened a small wooden box. He pulled out the locket and dangled it from his pointer finger.

"Maggie noticed the necklace and when I searched your bag and didn't see a box for it, I grabbed you one from my collection. It's safe, just like you are." He handed me the necklace and sat down at the foot of the bed. "So, is there a picture inside of it or just a pretty empty locket?"

"It was a gift from someone. There's a picture of us in it from the summer festival back home." I put the necklace on and pulled my hair through the chain. Both males looked at me intensely, as if I just said something horribly wrong. "What?"

"So, you're taken?" Damian asked from in front of the door. He crossed his arm and looked at Bastian, who had also gone rigid.

"I mean, technically no, because he hasn't asked me or any-thing." I looked down at my hands, twisting them in the blanket. It was a nice soft material, fluffy but not too fluffy. I looked at both of the males, like really looked at them. Damian's red hair was pulled back into a low ponytail, his beard was neat and kept, his red eyes danced in the light like pools of rubies, the muscles on his arms were wrapped in some type of tattoos. Bastian looked bored. His granite grey eyes turned to a molten silver when he caught me staring, his black hair pulled up into a man bun, tattoos covering his arms and neck, his beard wasn't as well kept but it was still nice. Gods, these men were gorgeous and highly attractive. *Stop staring, stop staring.*

I had to blink a few times and turned my attention back out the window. Sadly, Bastian wasn't about to let what he saw go. "See something you like?" He mused from the edge of the bed. "I mean, you have two attractive, muscular fae males in a room all to yourself. Your leg may not be one hundred percent, but I'm sure the two of us could hold you up. One in front of you, kissing your neck while the other holds you from behind, kissing your back." Heat flooded through my core and my breathing became heavier. Damian must've picked up where Bastian was going because he closed in on the left side of the bed, Bastian moving to the right.

Damian leaned over. "Or we could just position you on your side, him behind you, caressing you and kissing your back. Me in front of you, tasting those beautiful, luscious lips. They're a beautiful shade of red, you know. I wonder how they taste." He lowered his face to mine and smiled. My breath caught, my lips parting, wanting to respond. "Oh Bastian, she's speechless." He smiled, wrapping a strand of my blonde-blue hair around his finger, gently running his finger down my cheek, releasing the strand of hair. I reflectively arched into his touch, Bastian leaned in to whisper into my ear.

"Do you want to be touched, little Luna?" shivers rushed down my spine, a whimper of need escaping from my lips. Enough of an answer for them. Bastian lowered down on the bed behind me, slowly pulling back the blanket, revealing the gossamer silk white gown that someone had changed me into.

Damian's eyes turned hungry. He leaned close enough that our breath twined. Another whimper escaped from me. The more I whimpered, the hungrier his eyes became. Bastian ran his fingers up my side, trailing from my hip up to the side of my breast, his fingers grazing the flesh at the top of the gown. Damian lowered his lips to mine and placed a gentle kiss on my lips. They tasted of cinnamon and clove. If just his lips tasted this good, how would the rest of him taste?

Bastian pulled me onto my back, both of them moving onto each side of me, placing kisses along my jaw. Damian stopped and pulled back. Gazing down at me with a wicked grin, Bastian drew up to my lips. He kissed me once, twice. By the third kiss, I parted my lips for his tongue to devour me. He tasted of snow and pine, a delicious reminder of winter on the horizon. He plunged a hand behind my head and pulled me into the kiss and I let go of any reserve my brain was trying to have and I kissed him back, grabbing at his neck and pulling him in deeper.

Damian laughed. "Such a hungry little one." Bastian pulled back and looked down at me. My gown was slowly becoming see through with sweat from the heat we were radiating. He looked at Damian and smiled.

"You get one, I get the other?" He quipped, and Damian smiled. As if in answer, each brother dropped their heads to my breast and sucked hard on my nipples right through the fabric. Bastian twirled his tongue around the hardened peak while Damian nipped and pulled gently with his teeth. I was about to unravel at the sensation, the fabric becoming wet and rubbing against my sensitive breasts.

Release was soon to find me. As if sensing my need, both brothers bit down hard on my nipples, and I tumbled over the threshold of relief. Neither stopped until my heart stopped racing. This was a sensation I've never felt before and I wanted more.

Both of them pulled back before I could kiss them again. They sat up with a smug look of satisfaction on their faces. Bastian pulled the blanket back up over my chest to hide my now soaked gown, I groaned. The door opened not even a minute later, as the woman from this morning entered my room with lunch. I guess they knew we were about to have company.

Damian got up and grabbed the tray from her and nodded as she retreated out the door. He walked over to me and Bastian, still on the bed; I sat up letting the blanket fall to my waist as Damian set the tray on my lap. "Are you a good little one?" He smiled at me.

"I, uh.." I just nodded at them, not sure how to express my want, and looked at the tray of fruits and seared meat. They both laughed a deep, throaty laugh. "So, um, do you two always treat your guests like this?"

Bastian looked at me, his eyes still a molten silver, "No, you just intrigue us. Are you complaining, though?"

My cheeks heated, and I shook my head, shoving fruit in my mouth. Damian kissed the top of my head and sat back down on the bed. "Hopefully we can do that again in a more private setting." He winked at me, and I quickly looked away before my face betrayed me. They both just laughed, "Eat up little one, you're gonna need your energy." Bastian quipped as he bit at my ear. Oh gods, I was in trouble.

CHAPTER 22
LUNA

Damian and Bastian helped me out of the bed and into the chair that Maggie had sent up to my room. Bastian had pushed me out of the room and down the hall while Damian followed close behind. It was odd. I never got this kind of treatment from Virgil, or any other boy, for that matter. Virgil always told me I could do it on my own. Not in a mean way but more of a, you got this kind of manner. He loved me in his own way.

"I'm going to go see if Maggie has anything for your family. If she does, I'll head there and make the deliveries." Damian came up beside me and looked down at me, no hint of the devious behavior from earlier.

"Thank you. Can I write a letter for you to take for someone else?" He stiffened at the words someone else but nodded. I had to write to Virgil. As much as I wanted to say yes to him in the letter and tell him I love him more than the stars, something was different now. Maybe it was the fact that he was the only man to take an interest in me thanks to Luther, so I always thought he would be the one that no one else would dare want me. Clearly, that is not the case and now

I'm questioning if it is love I feel for Virgil or just want, need. Both of which he refused to give me after our first time. Aside from longing looks, a kiss here or there and hugs a plenty, there was nothing else. No dragging me into a broom closet to have his way with me, no sneaking into my room on the nights he stayed over. I tried constantly, but he always stopped me. He says he wants me, but maybe I'm not the right one for him.

Bastian stopped pushing the chair once we got to the bottom level of the Mor. He walked over to the front desk and retrieved a pen and a notepad and handed it to me. "Here, write your letter so Damian can go play delivery boy."

Slight guilt hit my stomach hard at the delivery boy comment. "You don't have to deliver this for me, Damian. I just don't know any other way around here to get a letter to him."

"It's fine." He said through gritted teeth. Bastian tightened his grip on the wheelchair. Shit, they didn't know I was writing to another man. I guess they had a right to be upset, but they don't know the full story. I turned my attention back to the paper.

Virgil,

I left for Mistveil at the request of my father for aid from the healers. I found the locket you left for me and the note. The locket is beautiful. Thank you. As far as your question, I don't know. Before I left, I would've said yes a thousand times, yes. I always wanted to be with you and saw myself as your wife somewhere far away from there. But I won't be back before you have to go off to war and things have changed. I got hurt on my way here and it's looking like I'll be here for a few weeks. But I don't even know if I want to come back at all if the healers send help before I'm better. What I'm saying is right now it's a no. Maybe our paths will cross again someday. Just be safe, please. Stay with Nox. He will help keep you safe and alive. I couldn't imagine losing you.

Love,

Luna

I folded the letter and handed it to Damian. "Please don't read it." He grabbed the letter and nodded.

"It's none of my business but, the guy you wrote this to, is he going to come for you?" Damian held up the letter and waved it. That was a fair question.

"No, Virgil has his orders, and he's an obedient captain of the Royal guard. He may love me, but he values what makes him money more." I wasn't wrong. Virgil wouldn't leave his post even if he wanted to. Orders were orders, is what he would always tell me. "He's heading to Galbranth in two days. If you miss him, just leave it at my house. Someone will get it to him." I looked at the front doors to the Mor, the city sprawling out in front of me. Excitement filled my body. For once in my life, I felt like I wasn't being depended upon. Hopefully Maggie could send something with Damian to help the graying with my family and I wouldn't have to return. Lilly could start living a life without everyone being a mother hen to her. Maybe my father could make up his absence from her life. They will be okay, they will live, and they will be okay.

"Alright, well then, I better get heading to Maggie and see what she has for me." Damian leaned down and kissed me on the top of my head then whispered in my ear, "Be good little Luna." He straighten and looked at Bastian, a simple nod from each other and Bastian was wheeling me out the front doors while Damian headed to Maggie. I called back to Damian.

"Thank you!" I heard him chuckle, but couldn't make out what he said in return.

"Where to little Luna?" Bastian asked me, wheeling me towards the gates of the Mor.

"Are you two going to continue calling me little Luna forever?" I snapped at him.

"Oh yes, your nose crinkles a little, but your eyes light up when we say it." He was wrong. He laughed, "Oh, the pouty look is very suiting, little Luna."

I crossed my arms and huffed a bit; he laughed deeper. "Let's get you to your temporary new home." I smiled softly. New home. This was going to be a new life, even if it was just a temporary escape.

CHAPTER 23
DAMIAN

What in the hell came over us back there? And who in the hell was this Virgil she writing to? She said technically she is single, which means that she's not married or dating him, but maybe she wants to be with him. The letter in my hand seemed to sing to me to read it. I knew better, though. The door to the high priestesses room was open, the sunlight dancing with the specks of dust in the air.

I knocked on the open door. "Come in." Maggie said from behind her desk. Vials of every color lined her table and shelves. Her eyes shifted up to see me over her half-rimmed glasses that were barely resting on the bridge of her nose. "I have the letter for her family ready. I'm working on instructions for the medicine I'm sending with you. It will not get rid of the graying immediately but, it will slowly start the recovery process." She pointed at two vials full of a green liquid. "If they are as lucky as she is, it won't take long for the graying to leave their systems. Her sister just needs to actually take it. Which, according to Luna, is going to be the difficult part." Maggie sighed.

"Is it really that simple that those vials will heal them?" I asked slightly in disbelief.

Maggie sighed and put her pen down to fully look at me. "Damian, your father could've ended these deaths decades ago when it started. I asked to set up spaces outside the human cities and towns to save them, but someone convinced him that their illnesses and diseases could affect us. If her mother had just come here instead of heading towards Mirith, she would've been healed already." She shook her head and went back to writing.

"Then none of us would have met her." The thought of that unsettled me, unlocking something old in my heart. Something not happy with that, though. "Have you ever experienced a feeling of rightness with someone you never met?" The question slipped out before I realized it. She didn't look up from her notes.

"Yes, it was a human from Fildery. He came here after a horrible hiking incident had broken both of his legs and one of his arms. His friends carried him here, begging for our help. His friends had to return home, but he had to stay here for several months to fully recover. I had just started my classes with the original high priestess at the time. She had me working day and night with him to get him fully healed. Once I saw him, I didn't want to leave his side. Your father was gracious enough to allow the man to try the descent. Luckily for me, he survived and has been my husband ever since." She smiled up at me, knowing why I asked.

"Gregor was human?!" I shouted, a little louder than I intended. My father gave him the challenge of the descent and granted him immortality to be with his love. Shocked was a massive understatement.

"Yes, and the way you ran in here last night with her in your arms. I know that feeling of terror that I saw in you. I saw it in Bastian this morning when I checked in on her. Have you heard of how the mating bond works?" She asked as she folded up the papers and slipped them into an envelope, writing the word *instructions* on it before sealing it. I've heard of the mating bond and witnessed it with my father and all our mothers, but I thought it to be rare.

"I know it's why my father is mated to five women. Each accepted the other as the bond kicked in. Hell, it's why Bastian and I are so close. Our mothers are sisters." I said to Maggie, it wasn't a secret. "But what I was always under the impression is that mating might not ever happen to my brothers and me. It's a rare thing."

She shook her head. "While yes, mates are considered rare in our realm, that is usually because most Fae are mates to humans who don't know a thing about it. Most are too afraid of us or stay away from us to know much of anything, so we never get the chance to meet them. If she is anything like I have gathered, she might just be very special." She smiled and handed me the two letters. She grabbed a satchel from the shelf and wrapped the two vials in cloth and put them in the bag, then took the letters and put them inside as well. "Go take these to her father and sister. Try not to make too big of a presence. You don't want the people in the town ignoring her family because they received aid from the Fae."

I nodded my thanks and headed out of the Mor and towards Celvenia. I knew what she meant. Dull down the Fae looks and look human. I got into the woods and took off. I'll shift my appearance when I get to town.

I reached the edge of town by nightfall. One perk of being fae is our speed. I thought long and hard on my way here about how I was going to change my appearance enough to make the people at ease with me being in town. I focused on changing my ears, making them rounder and smaller, pulling my canines back into my gums a little more. That probably hurt the most of all this. Last, my bright red eyes and hair would be a dead giveaway that I am not human. I focused on Luna's eyes in my head. The creamy dark chocolate brown, and let my eyes look like hers, changing my hair to a muted ginger red. That should do it. I stopped at the fork in the road and looked at the sapphire blooms; they reminded me of her. I picked one off the bush and popped it into the satchel. Thanks to military files, I knew where Luna lived and could head straight there.

I expected to be stopped by the guards at the gates, but they did nothing. They didn't even really acknowledge me. Now that was strange and also worrying. Pushing my way through the slight crowd, I made my way down the cobblestone streets towards the town square. It was beautiful for the most part, intricate street lamps, flags of greens, reds and golds decorated the streets and the amphitheater was lit up for the occasion this evening that Luna was talking about.

I managed to make my way through the crowded streets and down her street. The small iron gates leading to her home looked well kept. The house was lit up, which was a good sign. I walked to the front door and knocked.

A delicate ebony woman answered the door, "Can I help you?" She studied me, looking up and down, her dreads swaying gently.

"I've come here on an errand from Luna. I need to speak to her father and to Virgil." I stood there waiting for her rejection, but she moved and let me pass.

"Have a seat there," she pointed at a well-worn couch, and I took my seat. "Just be careful. Gunther's in a bad mood today." She headed to the back of the house. I looked around the living space. It was cozy. I heard coughing from down the hall. I think it's safe to say that was Lilly if Gunther was in the back of the house. I watched the woman as she made her way through the house and towards a door that must lead to his bedroom.

The fire in the hearth was warm. I wonder who would stay with Lilly and Gunther when she left for the evening. I hope this stuff works for them. Taking in the whole room, I noticed a cluster of paintings in the corner. A beautiful pink and purple sunset on one, and a meadow full of flowers on another. They were breathtaking, but before I could look any closer, a horrible sound got my attention.

A scream came from the back room. I jumped to my feet and ran toward the scream. The ebony woman stumbled out of the door sobbing.

"What's happened?" I tried to keep my voice calm as I looked past her into the room. The General looked asleep in the bed, but something smelled off.

"He's.... He's dead." She sobbed, dropping to her knees. I was too late to save him. My eyes looked down at the woman in front of me. I had to get her out of here and to the front room. I hoisted her up in my arms and walked her back to the sitting room. A tall delicate ivory skinned woman entered the house a moment later with bags of what smelled like fruits of some sort. She took one look at the girl on the couch and then at me with an accusatory look.

"Kira, what's going on here?" the woman spoke with a tone of urgency in her voice. I stepped forward.

"My name is Damian. I came here on behalf of Luna to see her father and sister. However, my timing was not perfect. I got here too late." I looked at the woman as her head turned to the back room. I stepped into her line of sight. Although he looked asleep, I could smell the reek of death creeping out of the room. "Is Lunas sister here?"

Kira looked up at me. "Yes, she's in the first room on your right, down the hallway." She glanced down the hall and back at me.

"Thank you." I said to Kira. Her eyes were glassy, the tears still streaming down her cheeks. I turned to head towards Lilly's room

The ivory woman was in front of me in a blink of the eye, blocking me from going down the hallway. "Are you serious Kira? How do you know he isn't here to harm her?" She shouted.

"Harper, he showed up, asking to speak to Gunther. If Luna sent him-" Harper waved her hand at Kira like a child not wanting to be told no.

"It doesn't mean he isn't here to do harm." She puffed her chest out at me and I tried hard not to laugh at the thought that she thinks she can stop me.

"I have a letter from Luna to a man named Virgil. I have to deliver that as well if you two could point me in his direction. First, I have to give this letter from the high priestess of Mistveil to someone in Luna's family. Since her father is no longer with us, it needs to go to her sister." I pulled the letters out and Harper snatched them and opened the one addressed to the family, scanning the letter quickly.

"How in the hell did she get hurt?!" Harper exclaimed at me, handing the letter to Kira on the couch.

"She was riding her bike down a dirt path in the middle of the night and got attacked by a Borg. Luckily, I was following her and was able to help get her away from it. Before you ask, I wasn't stalking her. I saw a light in the cottage in Wardveil and I thought it was odd, so I went to check it out." I had to lie a bit, so they didn't figure out too much.

"At least she made it to the healers. Thanks to you. So, thank you. But you have another letter in your hand, what it is?" she pointed at the third letter, the one labeled instructions.

"The high priestess listened to Luna's plea for help for her family. This letter is instructions for these." I reached into the satchel and pulled out the two vials. "The high priestess said these will do the trick to rid the body of the graying. It won't be instant, but one vial will do the trick. The instructions are in here." I handed over the instruction letter and watched Harper speed read it. She held her hand out, and I handed her a vial.

"I'll go give this to Lilly and tell her about her father. Please let Luna know." With that, she went down the hall and into Lilly's room.

"I have to go to the barracks and tell her brother. I can take the letter to Virgil for you. Don't worry, I won't read it. Tell Luna I miss her. I wasn't able to see her before she left. Gunther told Harper and me about his request. If this stuff works for Lilly, I'll leave a message at the cottage. Tell her I said go and finally live her life. There's nothing here for her once Lilly is better." Kira sighed deeply and looked up at me. "Luna has played mother and care giver since their mother left. She lost her childhood and has done everything for everyone else. She deserves to live." Kira stood and took the letter out of my hand for Virgil and headed towards the door.

"Kira wait," I called to her. "Do you need help with Gunther's body? I can help move him if you need me to."

"No, Luther would be mad if we had someone else move his father. Virgil, him and the General can do the heavy lifting. Just get back to our Luna. I'll send word in two days to the cottage." She grabbed the handle and opened the door.

"I'll be there." I nodded and followed her out the door. How was I going to tell Luna about her father? This wasn't going to be an easy thing to do. I headed back towards the main gates of Celvenia, I'll be back in my wolf and back home to her soon.

CHAPTER 24
LUNA

Bastian wheeled me into the foyer of the castle. It was beautiful. Marble flooring with plush blue carpeting, throughout the room the couches and chairs were arranged is small little groups, a fireplace on the far-right wall with a little chess table setup in front of it. I looked around the room, taking in the breathtaking paintings, the chandelier that hung in the center of the room. It was a large crystal chandelier with multiple tear drops falling in different hues; it was mesmerizing the way the light hit each drop.

"Would you like to see your room?" Bastian leaned down and whispered in my ear, chills running down my spine as he spoke.

"If it's anything like this room, you may have to force me to leave." I joked, but in all seriousness, this room alone was magnificent.

"Oh, I think you'll like it. Fennik assumed the color choice for your room but if you want it changed at all, just let someone know. There is a maid who is well versed in healing who will help you recover while you're here." Bastian pushed me through the foyer and down a wide hallway. Small lights lined each side as we walked. The blue carpet flowed into the hall in front of me. It looked like this hall was hardly ever used. He stopped and walked around me at the final door at the end of the hall. "I hope you like living like a Princess little Luna."

He pushed open the door to reveal a large stone room with a cathedral ceiling, arched with wood around an open balcony looking out over the forest and towards the mountains. The room had a large low-lying bed covered in white and purple blankets, a fireplace in front of it and two purple cushioned chairs. The night tables by the bed had what looked like small antler lamps on them. The dresser next to the bed was a beautiful cherry oak, with small engravings of what looked like sapphire blooms on each drawer. The room was beyond extraordinary.

"It's beautiful." I gasped. Bastian wheeled me into the room and led me to the bed. He put his arms out, and I grabbed at his wrists to help me stand. Before I could steady myself on my own, he had me up and in his arms, carrying me on to the bed. His pine and snow scent filling my nose. It was intoxicating how he smelled. My mind starting trailing back to this morning and a heat began building in my core. He laid me on the bed and stared at me. Could the fae scent need and desire? His eyes turned back to the pools of molten silver from this morning. He licked his lips just slightly, and I quivered a little under that heavy stare.

"If I don't leave this room right now, the gentleman that I was raised to be will go right out that window." He looked at me but didn't make a move towards the door.

"What if I don't want that, gentleman?" I asked through the heated desire rising in me. His eyes stared a hole in me, as if they were undressing me and the gods knew I wanted that.

"May I sit?" he gestured to the bed, asking with a sense of urgency in his tone. I patted the bed in response, and he peered at the door. He had left it open. "One second." he walked over and shut and locked the door. No interruptions, good.

He climbed on the bed next to me and reached a hand up to my cheek. The coolness of his skin set my own on fire. I leaned into his touch, and he shuddered. Trailing my hand up his arm, I traced his muscles, slowly mapping out each detail. I leaned closer to him, our breath tangling together, lips parting.

"Say the words, little Luna, and it's yours." Bastian was waiting patiently, but I couldn't wait.

"Please," I whispered back at him, waiting for him to take me, the need becoming heavier with every passing second.

"Please, what sweet one?" He smiled, and my core throbbed at the sight of that devilish grin.

"Please take me," I breathed out, my body on the verge of taking him if he kept teasing.

"Thank the gods!" He let out a groan and plunged his hands into my hair, gently pulling me into a deep kiss. His tongue nudged at my lips, and I parted them for him. His kiss was deep, tasting of snow and something sweet, his tongue learning the movements of my own.

He pulled back gently and looked down at my clothes, pulling down the thin straps to expose my breasts to him. The cool air caressed my skin, perking my heavy breasts up for him. He dipped his head down, nipping and licking at the sensitive rose-colored flesh. I couldn't help the moan that escaped me. I tugged at his shirt. He broke his attention long enough to send his shirt flying across the room. I moved further up on the bed, spreading my legs, so he could settle down between them. He looked as if he could feast on me. I pulled up my dress to expose my thighs a little more to him. His eyes flashed up at me and the grin set in place.

"Now that is a beautiful sight," he placed soft quick kisses up my thighs, stopping right at the thin scrap of now wet fabric covering my slit. He got up on his knees and undid his pants, pulling them down to his ankles. His thickness bounced as if being set free from a cage. I couldn't hide the gasp that came out of me at the sight of it. His length was stunning. I wanted to wrap my lips around it, my mouth watering at the thought.

I reached my hand toward him and rub my fingers gently up his shaft. He trembled at my touch. The head becoming shiner the more

I touched it. I leaned forward and licked my tongue from the base of his shaft to the tip of his head. It tasted like fresh snow and salt. He put his hand in my hair and gazed down at me. Taking that as my go ahead, I opened my mouth and rested his head in between my lips. His eyes widened, and he grinned. He gently grabbed my hair into a ponytail and guided his length into my mouth. He tasted amazing. I picked up my pace, up and down. He tugged my hair gently and pulled my head back to where I had to look him in the eyes.

"Have you been on a tonic?" He asked me and I knew what he meant. I nodded my head in answer. "Good. I promise I'll be gentle."

He laid me down and pulled the dress up past my hips, gripping the undergarment and tearing it away to reveal myself to him. He settled between my legs, the head of his thickness pressing gently at my entrance. I pushed my hips up in need and he obliged, pushing gently into me until he was fully sheathed inside me. He felt amazing. He slowly pulled back just before pushing back into me with little force. I gripped the sheets with my fingers; he continued to pump in and out of me, getting deeper and deeper with each thrust. He gripped my hips and pulled me closer to him, seating me fully on him. I was coming undone; he held me onto him as he pushed in deeper, letting me find full release on him before he came undone with me.

He laid me back down, still fully seated in me, letting me come back down to reality. He pulled out and laid with his head on my bare breasts. Our breathing slowed and became normal again. I was waiting for him to just clean up and leave like Virgil did, but he didn't. He laid with me until I fell asleep.

CHAPTER 25
LUNA

I don't know what time he left or even how I got cleaned up and changed. Truthfully, I didn't care; I was on cloud nine. That was entirely different from my first time with Virgil. I rolled over in bed and saw a small silver ring with a small onyx stone set in the middle of it. I reached over and picked it up off the table and rolled onto my back, holding the ring up and examining it. The band was a slender silver piece with a vine like engraving around the sides meeting up to an onyx stone in the center. I slipped it onto my middle finger, and it fit perfectly. Did Bastian leave this for me?

I could hear muffled footsteps and murmuring from down the hall. I sat up in bed, looking down at the purple lace gown I was now dressed in. I slept like the dead last night. When was the last time I slept so well? A knock came at the door, three soft knocks. "Come in." I said, a little louder than I intended.

"Good morning Luna." Fennik said as he came bouncing into the room, followed by Damian, Bastian, and two others I didn't know. "This is Valyn and Niklaus, our two other brothers who share this home with us." He pointed at each of them and they both nodded. All the brothers were very attractive, muscular and tattooed, like the gods crafted them by hand.

"It's nice to meet you both. I would bow, but I'm kind of stuck in this bed." I offered a smile and a slight bow of the head, to which they both nodded back. "Damian, how did my family react to the news that I wouldn't be home right away?"

He looked down, and Bastian gave him a reassuring pat on the back. "Luna, I don't know how to tell you this but, I was too late to get the medicine to your father. I met Harper and Kira, though. Harper gave Lilly the medicine, and I will meet with Kira tomorrow evening at your family's cottage to get the update from her on Lilly's condition." He looked at me with sorrow in his eyes.

I sat there in shock, tears rolling down my face that I barely even felt. Nox was right, my home was filled with death. Maybe he even knew before I did. I felt the bed lower to my left and looked up to find Bastian sitting beside me, wiping the tears from my eyes. "Do you know if he suffered?"

"Kira said he was grumpy earlier in the day. But he looked peaceful. I heard her scream and ran to check on her. She took your other letter with her to the barracks to inform your brother. She also wanted me to tell you, if the medicine works for Lilly, not to come home. To go live your life and that you deserve it." Damian pulled up a chair to the right of the bed and grabbed my hand. "I am so sorry I wasn't fast enough."

"No, please don't be sorry. As long as my sister got the medicine, that's all that matters." I said the words and meant them. I loved my father, but he wasn't always kind, and he had a full life. Lilly still has a full life ahead of her.

"Your friend seems kind of rude, if you ask me." Niklaus, the tall blonde-haired male, said from the doorway.

Valyn smacked him in the stomach and came to the foot of my bed. "Ignore him. He can be an ass. From what my brothers have said about you, you seem like the caregiver who needs a break." He smiled at me and dear gods, these brothers all had heart melting smiles.

Fennik took up a spot next to Valyn at the foot of the bed and glanced at me, then looked at his brothers on either side of me. "Luna, are you going to be okay? We wanted to come see you before Nik and I left to go speak to our father about the war you spoke of."

I gazed up at Fennik, "If I'm being honest, where it hurts me to know I wasn't there for him." I sighed deeply, thinking through my next words, "I won't say it's a relief or a burden lifted. But I'm glad he's no longer suffering. He had a full life. Damian, thank you for getting the medicine to my sister. She has a whole life ahead of her because of you and Maggie, and I am eternally grateful for you both."

Damian bowed his head. "How about one of us carry you to the dining hall? You should eat." Damian, Bastian and oddly enough Valyn all drew up close to me at the word carry. I stared blankly at them all.

"How about I use the chair, so you don't drop me?" I said to them with a bit of a forced smile.

Three of the brothers glanced at each other. Fennik backed out of the way, but it was Niklaus who chimed in from the door. "You've done it now. Enjoy being passed off down the hallway just to prove to you they won't drop you." He turned out the doorway and started down the hall, with Fennik following behind him. Bastian gripped me under my thighs and supported my back, and pulled me into his arms.

"I meant it! I want the chair!" I protested, but the boys just laughed. Bastian leaned in close to my ear.

"You're not getting out of my arms, little Luna. Not until I say so. Especially after last night." He looked at my hand and smiled. "It looks good on you."

"So, you did leave it for me," I whispered back to him.

"I brought it back this morning. I didn't think you wanted to wake up next to me snoring in your ear," Valyn and Damian were already in the hall. Bastian placed a kiss on my forehead. "We have a few things we need to talk about later."

We entered the hallway and before I could respond to Bastian; I was being pulled out of his arms by Valyn. I was stunned silent as he supported my weight in his arms. Bastian and Damian looked on edge. Valyn smiled at his brothers and started walking with me down the hall. They followed close behind.

"Well now Luna, you seem to be very intriguing. Has anyone ever told you that your eyes resemble the flowing chocolate from a waterfall?" He asked me so boldly. I shook my head. Was he flirting with me? Why are three fae princes so interested in me? Not complaining, but definitely curious.

"Don't think you can keep her all to yourself, Valyn." Damian piped in from behind us.

"Do you like the ocean?" Valyn smelled of sea salt and fresh pineapples. His tan skin gave off the vibe that he was definitely someone who loves the sun and the sea.

"I've never been to the ocean, only the Lake in Mirith as a kid." I admitted. I've never seen the sandy shores of the islands or even on our continent.

"Well, that just won't do. How about after breakfast we find you swimming attire and take you to the beach? I'll get it cleared by Maggie before we go. The water should help with your healing," Valyn smiled.

"Okay. I would love to see what the ocean looks like. Maybe I'll see a Mer if I'm lucky." I beamed from ear to ear. We were told stories as children about the fae known as mer and how beautiful they were.

"You might want to rethink meeting them." Damian said as we rounded the corner at the end of the hall and headed across the foyer. He stopped Valyn and pulled me into his arms. Bastian followed closely and within touching distance.

"Why is that? I heard they're lovely and beautiful." I'm beginning to think my curiosity might get the best of me here.

"Oh, they are," Valyn mused. "They're also deadly vicious creatures who've lured men and women to their deaths."

A shudder ran through my bones. "Don't scare her before breakfast, asshole." Bastian said, as he reached his hand toward mine. "You will be fine. Valyn may be a dick, but he won't let the creatures of his realm hurt you. It would be terrible publicity."

"Oh, come on, terrible publicity?" He laughed. "Truth be told, there hasn't been a mer sighting in about a decade. Either way, publicity or not. I won't let anything happen to you." Valyn looked me dead in the eyes and my heart began to race. His turquoise eyes looked like raging water, his jaw clenched as he turned from me towards Fennik and Niklaus. Suddenly, the three princes around me got closer, as if protecting me from the other two. I must be reading into it. I shook my head.

"Breakfast is served," Fennik smiled widely at me and opened the door to a huge dining room with the table full of delectable smelling food. My stomach rumbled, and Damian set me at the head of the table. I was starving. Each prince took a seat, Bastian and Damian on my right, and Valyn on my left. Fennik sat next to Valyn and Niklaus took a seat at the other head of the table staring a hole right into me.

CHAPTER 26
VALYN

If he doesn't stop looking at her like that, I'm going to rip his eyes out. The smell of Bastian all over her is already driving my senses insane. I am very impressed, however, that she hasn't caved under the stare of Niklaus.

"Can I help you?" she snapped at him. My interest is now fully piqued. Nik was used to always getting any girl with just a smile, but she doesn't seem interested in the slightest. His blood must be boiling. I had to stifle a laugh.

"You wreak of my brother and I'm curious what interest he has in a weak human like you. Or should I say, what they all see in you?" He looked at Bastian, Damian, and me. Bastian and Damian had their teeth bared slightly, but she just looked at Nik and smiled.

"I'm only weak because I messed my leg up. Trust me, I am more than capable of putting you on your ass when I'm healed up." She reached out for the plate of strawberries and grapes. I gladly grabbed the plate and handed it to her. Fennik went ghost white at her comments towards Nik. He wouldn't talk so boldly back like that. Yet this human in front of me was so bold that it made not just me perk up.

"You think you can beat me? I am stronger than you. I am immortal. Let's face it, once they get over the *newness* of you, my brothers will toss you aside. You're just a shiny new-" Niks words were cut off as a plate went sailing at his head. I can't tell if it was Bast or Damian who threw it, but Bast was seething up out of his chair.

"Don't you dare speak to her like that!" He was in Niks face and had his hand around Niks throat. I jumped up and grabbed Bastian's arm.

"Probably not the best idea." I looked Bast in the eyes and he let go.

"Speak like that to her again or about her and I think you'll have to fight off not just me, but those two as well." Bast backed off and sat back down next to Luna. Her hand slid to his, and she grabbed it, giving it a little squeeze. He settled into the chair and kept his focus on her.

I walked back over to my seat and looked at Damian. "You good over there?" He was still burning holes into Niks skull with his eyes.

"I'll be fine once I eat." He started piling different pasties and fruits on his plate. Grabbing a cheese Danish, he put it on Luna's plate. "You'll like those chef makes amazing pastries."

"I really like sweets. We couldn't really get them back home. At least not the good sweets." she giggled, and it was probably the cutest thing ever.

"You have until next week to find somewhere to be besides here. Let's go Fennik." He grabbed Fennik by the collar but when I made to move, he waved me off.

"Nik, remember you don't own this home and you're not the oldest. She will be here until Maggie says she is better. If you try anything, I will see to it personally that you will have to stay in your own realm, only being allowed here for formal meetings." I said. I may not be the oldest, but Damian was. I fell in second, but at least I had more pull with our father.

"You can't do that to me, and you know it." He glared at me, flexing his fingers in a ball.

"He can't, but I can," Damian spoke without even looking up from his plate. Nik shut his mouth and stormed out of the room.

"I'm really sorry about all of this Luna," Fennik gave an apologetic glance at Luna before running off after the idiot hot head. I turned back around to her and my brothers.

"Well, that was a very interesting breakfast. I'm going to go check in with Maggie real fast to make sure she is okay with you heading to the beach for a bit. If so, I will come back with a nice little outfit for you." I smiled at her and headed out. I would not let Niks foul mood ruin my plans for today.

LUNA

"Okay, so what in the world was that all about?" I looked at Damian and Bastian, both of them now eating as if they hadn't eaten in days.

"Nik thinks he owns the place and since you didn't drop, you dress to the floor upon him entering your room this morning. That must mean something's wrong with you." Bastian chuckled and winked at me.

"He's used to getting all the girls and us not even getting a second glance when he is around." Damian said between mouthfuls of food.

I picked at the pastries on my plate, pushing the fruit around. "Would it be best if I just go back to the Mor and stay there until I'm done healing? I don't want to be a burden or the reason you all fight."

They both stopped eating and looked at me. "Do not think we are making you leave. You will stay here, heal up and if you want to go back to Celvenia when you are better. As much as we wouldn't want that, we would take you home. If you instead chose to stay here in Mistveil, we would find you a place to live if you didn't want to stay here. You are welcome here. His comments, however, are not." Damian said with authority.

Bastian smiled at me, "I do, however, think that you and all of us have something to talk about once we get back with Valyn."

My cheeks flushed as they looked at me and smiled. I put a piece of the Danish in my mouth and immediately it melted in my mouth. The sweetness and tartness was a perfect blend. The fluffiness of the pastry itself was divine. I closed my eyes and just enjoyed the taste. It was perfect.

"I told you, you'd like it," Damian said, breaking me out of my daze. I opened my eyes as he was putting another one on my plate. "This one is strawberry and cream. It's one of my favorites."

"Thank you," I said as I cut the Danish in quarters. The smell was heavenly. Whoever the chef is, I need to ask them for more. I took the first bite and again I melted. The strawberries were perfect, sliced into thin slices. The cream cheese used was fluffed perfectly, the sweet and tart was perfectly balanced.

"That face right there is the cutest." Bastian chuckled. "I guess you really do like sweets."

I glared at him, then glanced at Valyn's plate. "Wait, Valyn didn't eat."

"Don't worry Luna, Valyn will eat. This probably would've been his second breakfast any ways." Damian folded his napkin and put it on his plate.

Bastian and I followed suit. "Are you ready to go? I'm going to go check in with Maggie about your medicine." Damian looked at me. I nodded and tried to get myself out of the chair, but Bastian was there quicker that I could more and scooped me up into his arms. I enjoyed walking, but I think I could get used to this. I smiled to myself.

CHAPTER 27
BASTIAN

Carrying Luna back to her room, I held her close to my chest, breathing in her vanilla and citrus scent. The slight hint of something else lingered around her. I just couldn't place the smell.

"You said you grew up going to the lake in Mirith. Can I ask why that was?" I asked as casually as I could. I want to learn as much about here as I can.

"My mother worked in service to Lord Drake since well before Luther was born. I actually was born in Mirith technically. My mother wasn't able to travel back home to Celvenia to have me. I didn't actually know that Mirith wasn't my home until I was about three." She smiled, but it didn't last long. A shadow covered her eyes, and I didn't like the look.

"Why so long?" Could it be because she was born on fae land that she has that subtle scent of ethereal wind to her?

"My father came and took us home. He was away at war when I was born and Luther was with my father's side of the family in Belhaven. We didn't hear much from them after the war. My uncle wasn't happy with my father's involvement in it." We finally got back to her room. I looked between the bed and the couch.

"I know you don't want to be in a bed all day and hopefully you won't be. For now, how about we sit outside on your patio?" I offered the option. She looked down at her attire and then out the door.

"Is there any clothing here that won't show me off like a lady of the night?" Her cheeks turned red. I set her down on the couch by the fireplace and opened a drawer. Rummaging through the clothes that Damian and Fennik ransacked from some shop, I found a pair of black loose cotton sweatpants and a light pink t-shirt and pulled them out.

"Don't blame me if these don't fit you. Damian and Fennik went shopping and grabbed what they thought would fit. Would you like help?" *Please say yes! Please say yes!*

She smiled at me. "I might need help with the one leg of the pants, but I got everything else."

Dammit, oh well. One leg was better than nothing at all. I shrugged to myself and handed her the pink top. She pulled off the lace dress she was wearing, and I immediately forgot that I didn't put any undergarments back on her last night. She sat there completely exposed, and my heart started racing. The urge to capture her breasts in my teeth was strong. The little gasp that escaped her lips was breathy. I guess she didn't realize it either.

The door knob turned and in came Damian with a bottle of water in one hand and a red vial of something in the other. Valyn was behind him bantering on about something. I instinctively jumped in front of her as they both stopped dead in their tracks and looked past me to the luscious, curvy naked woman behind me.

"It's not what you think. She is just changing." I quickly snatched a sheet off the bed and held it up with my arms.

Valyn stepped forward first, a twisted grin plastered across his face. "Oh, come now, it's not like we didn't just glimpse her fully naked before that thin sheet was thrown up."

He grabbed the sheet and threw it onto the bed. His eyes lit with excitement as Luna's cheeks were a full flushed pink. Damian growled from where he stood.

"Luna, I'm supposed to give you this to help you with leg pain today, but now I think it will be an aid in helping you with another type of pain." Damian licked his lips and pushed past me, kneeling at her feet. My brother kneeled to no one, not even our father. Valyn looked at me with a bewildered expression. I felt a sudden tug in my mind to get close to her.

Like instincts taking over, I was at her side a heartbeat later, Valyn dropping on the other side. Damian had her legs spread wide before him, her entrance slick and puffy. His hooded gaze met hers and I saw it there, the spark in his eyes that matched mine.

"Nothing will happen without your say so." He spoke to her like he was in a trance, and her eyes locked in on him like Valyn and I weren't even here. She nodded her head, and he smirked, but it was Valyn who spoke next.

"No little one, you need to use your words." He ran his fingers through her hair, and she rested her head into his hand. I felt like I should pull away a bit to let her decide. I went to move off to the side of the couch a little farther away, but her hand reached out for me, and I couldn't refuse her.

"I won't leave if you don't want me to." I whispered in her ear. She tore her eyes away from Damian for a split second for me to see the swirl of light gold flick into her eyes. She looked at Valyn and then back at Damian.

"Please don't leave me," she whispered and right there my heart snapped into place, a sense of rightness filled me. I would not leave her, not now, not ever.

"I'll never leave you." We said as one. For that moment, everything seemed so right. The world just clicked into place. Her eyes focused on Damian once more, and she whimpered as he gazed down at her.

"Please," she whispered. That was it, the teether on Damian unleashed.

LUNA

The world spun around me in colors of crimson and violet and silver. Everything just felt right. The word please escaped from my lips and my world shot to the stars. Damian began feasting on me like I was the air he needed to breathe.

Tasting me and drinking me all in, I pulled Bastian to me and started kissing him passionately, my other hand grabbing at Valyn's shirt. I didn't know what was coming over me, but I liked it. Bastian pulled back, smiling, turning my face to Valyns. He bit my lower lip, and I gasped at the light pain. Valyn tasted like pineapple and sea salt. It was delicious. Damian moaned into my entrance, taking long licks teasing me.

"Sounds like someone is getting jealous," Valyn laughed a little, pulling out of our kiss. I missed his lips against mine already. He reached down and pulled Damian up by his hair. "If you want to taste her lips so bad then get up here and switch with me."

Damian and Valyn quickly swapped placed. Damian gripped my hair and pulled me into a kiss that made me see stars. Tasting myself on him turned me on more than I expected. Valyn dipped between my legs and kissed up my thighs to my entrance, slowly licking my slit from bottom to top. He slid his hands from my knees up to my thighs and back down; I lifted my hips at the electric rush.

"Now I feel left out," Bastian whined and nipped at my shoulder. I leaned my head back at him and smiled as Damian kissed my neck.

"Then do something about it." I said between pants and moans.

"As you wish," he smiled at me and pushed Damian and Valyn back off of me. I whimpered at the coldness that it left me with. Bastian laid me out on the couch and put my legs up towards my head. A giggle escaped me as they each looked at me. Bastian looked at them and all bets were off, or should I say, all pants came off.

I couldn't even compare them. Each brother had an amazing length, and they stood around me, all at attention. "So who goes first?" I couldn't help but ask as if I had done this a million times. My confidence was extremely high for my lack of experience. The males looked at each other and smiled.

"We're all going first." Valyn smiled at me and the surprise on my face once I realized what he meant must have been great for them, because they all laughed.

Valyn gripped me up off the couch and headed towards the bed, laying me down in the center, Damian taking up the right side of the bed while Bastian came up to the left. My hands immediately went for Damian and Bastians full, velvety soft length, the thickness feeling so soft on my palms.

Valyn lowered himself onto his knees and spread my legs wide for him. "I'll be gentle, little one." He kissed my slit, then ran the head of his length against my entrance. I lifted my hips, and he took that as his permission. He gripped my hips and pushed himself in. The moan escaping my lips became muffled as I took Damian's length between them, trailing my tongue up the thick veined length from balls to the tip of his head. Valyn and Damian kept pace with each other, my other hand trying to keep pace up and down on Bastian's hard member. Faster and harder they pumped into me, Damian thickening in my mouth. A salty sweetness leaked out of the tip. He grabbed my hair and pulled my head back, so my eyes met his as he released his warmth inside my mouth. I took it all and swallowed it. The taste of him, a salty sweetness.

Valyn started pumping harder into me, pulling back slowly to the head, then pushing fast and deep into me. I wanted to be seated deep on top of him; I ground my hips against him and felt myself riding for relief. Valyn picked up my need and pounded deep into me. My world began spinning. The ecstasy of him inside of me felt magnificent. My need had me throbbing about to explode. He thrusted once more, gripping my hips and pulling me closer. I fell through my release; Valyn thrusted faster, his breath getting heavier. Right before he found his, he whispered, "Luna." And spilled into me.

I turned my attention to Bastian and brought his length into my mouth, bringing it in and out with my hand as extra guidance. I wanted more. I wanted to taste Bastian on my tongue. I took him all the way into my mouth, pleased by the moans that escaped from him. He looked down at me with a smile on his face and winked. I put him in my mouth as far as he could go and twirled my tongue up his length as I pulled my head up. I picked up my pace and took him all the way back down my throat, slightly choking a bit on his length. He let out a beautiful moan as he poured his release into me, and I drank it all up.

I gazed at the males now all in my bed. Each of them was breathing heavily. Our bodies curled up on top of each other. Valyn curled up on my thighs, Damian laid down on one side of me as Bastian lowered himself onto the bed. Our breathing twined, and the world felt like it was holding onto time itself for us.

CHAPTER 28
DAMIAN

Watching her take me and my brothers was amazing, her body laid glistening on the bed. Valyn laid out on her thighs, panting at the bottom of the bed, Bastian beside her curled up to her half in a daze. This whole thing with her felt so right. I don't want to lose this feeling, but I know I had to bring things back to reality. I looked over next to the couch and saw the vial of medicine still sealed on the floor. Thank the gods it didn't open up. I wouldn't know how to explain to Maggie how it got spilled. I pulled myself away from her and got up. She whimpered a little, her eyes tracking my every movement. I walked over and picked the vial up off the floor along with the water bottle and walked back over to the bed.

"I hate to be the one to kill the mood, but Luna, you need to take this." She looked at me with hazy eyes and smiled, sitting up. Bastian groaned as she moved but put his head on her lap. Valyn shifted on her thighs. I uncorked the vial and handed it to her. She took it and sniffed it.

"Why does medicine here not smell and taste gross?" she asked as she downed the vial of liquid.

"Does medicine not taste good where you're from?" Valyn asked her, his breathing was finally evening out. Luna just shook her head no and looked down at Bastian and Valyn, and her smile grew.

"They didn't leave." She whispered to herself, and we all looked at her. Pretty sure we weren't supposed to hear that, but we definitely did.

"That's not the first time you said something about us leaving you. Please don't tell me someone abandoned you after sex." Valyn was now on his side, head propped up on a fist. Bastian laid on his back with his head still in her naked lap. Thankfully this bed was huge.

She looked out the window and sighed deeply. "Well, yeah actually. My first time I thought was magical, but he left me quickly afterwards. I was alone with my thoughts, and I thought that was what sex was until last night." She blushed and looked down at Bastian. Obviously, we all could scent her on him and him on her, but I don't think she knows we can scent her like that. The scent of her raising desire can be overwhelming sometimes and need and want to take her is strong.

"Well, whoever that ass was, he needs to be left behind. You shouldn't have been left afterwards. Not unless you're a lady of the night and that you are definitely not." Bastian said to her, and I seconded his words. Valyn moved up her body, laying himself a top of her. He gazed into her eyes and kissed her.

"You will never be left alone, not after sex, not after sleeping, not even after an argument. We will talk it out and move on. Hope you enjoyed your alone time before you met us, because you're stuck with us now." He winked at her, and I sat on the bed next to them all.

Tears rolled down her cheeks. Bastian and I caught them and wiped them away. "That makes me so happy to hear. I thought I was happy back home, creating this life in my mind with a man who asked me to be his girl through a letter. I am genuinely happy and scared all at the same time." She smiled at us and pulled us all into a big sweaty hug.

Valyn got up off the bed and walked over to the couch, grabbing our pants and throwing them at us. He grabbed the pink t-shirt and the black sweatpants and laid them on the bed for her. He put the sweatpants around her ankles and Bastian lifted her legs and hips as Valyn guided the pants up to her hips. She grabbed the shirt, and I helped her get it on over her head.

"No undergarments?" She asked.

"You wish," Bastian replied, as he kissed her cheek.

"Well, we may have to forgo the beach today. It's already getting late, and we all need food now." He laughed and wasn't wrong as we heard her tummy make a rumbling sound. She busted out laughing, and it was the best sound in the world. Bastian and I pulled our pants on, and he grabbed the wheelchair from the far side of the room.

"Let's go eat." We got her in the chair and pushed her out of the room and down the hallway. Today was the start of something new, something pure.

CHAPTER 29
NOX

It has been three days since we got here. I sent word to the General about what had happened and that I was required to stay with Captain Crawley. Yes, I was technically in *enemy* territory but, I still needed to speak with my father. Something didn't seem right about this war.

Bethany has been keeping Virgil company during the few waking hours he's had. Nothing major but trying to see how his breathing was doing, and what his pain level was. I think in three days he only has been awake for maybe 6 hours. He eats some and then sleeps. I've seen him conscious maybe twice. The pain he must be experiencing has to be horrible. I've been through some stuff myself, but I've never been stabbed in the chest.

My father was home today, and I could get away from Listhrum for a bit. The red banners waved in the ocean breeze between the marble pillars heading to the throne room. Red and gold banners and runners were everywhere. I walked down the hallway towards the outer throne room that looked over the Kilspur ocean. My father was sitting on the throne looking out over the water. His bright blue and grey hair danced in the wind.

"Something is on your mind, my son." He spoke matter-of-factly. He always seemed to know when something was wrong. It freaked me out a bit.

"Well, a few things are going through my mind right now." I said, coming up beside him looking out over the water myself. It was calm.

"Go on." He said, looking at me, waiting for me to continue.

"General Rothsberg is claiming there is a war about to be waged on our lands between us and Mistveil. He's demanding I ride at the head of the dragon legion with General Gunther's son Luther. Honestly, I really want to drop into the depths and watch him drown. And now because of Luther, I have a Captain at Lithstrum who I promised to keep safe for Luna, which I clearly broke that promise. Honestly, I'm in really deep and I don't know what side is up anymore." I sighed into my hands.

"As far as I know, Harold and I are on good terms. I'll send word to Mistveil about the news you bring, so we can sort this out. As for the promise you made Luna, what all did you say to her?" My father's eyes lingered on me longer than I liked.

"She doesn't know anything. I may have slipped in anger and told Luther that she's my sister too, but that was only because he had a knife at my throat, thinking I was going to harm her." I signed heavily,

"My promise to her was to protect the man whose now in Listhrum. Currently Bethany is with him, healing a hole in his chest, courtesy of Luther. I failed her already."

My father turned to me, and looked up, "You didn't fail her, Nox. The boy made it here alive. Thank the gods the wind brought you here swiftly."

He was right; I somehow managed to keep my promise as long as he stayed alive. He saved my life and in return I brought him somewhere that could heal him up and hopefully save his life. "I want to bring Luna here. I don't think she is safe in Celvenia."

My father just laughed. "I don't think you need to worry about her, Nox. You might see her sooner than you think." He rose from his throne, hugged me, and headed back into the castle with a smile on his face. Sometimes I wonder if he ever takes anything seriously.

I looked out over the Kilspur. I really hope she was safe, and that he was right. I need to tell her what happened before she sees Luther again. I sent a silent prayer up to Vanalli and headed back inside. It was going to be a long day.

CHAPTER 30
LUNA

It had been a week since I left Celvenia and started this weird journey. Damian received word from Kira that the medicine Maggie sent was working wonders for Lilly. It made my heart sing to hear that she was doing better. Maggie was letting me work on standing up and putting pressure on my legs. I could walk around the room finally. It was slightly painful, but I could steady myself without one of the princes grabbing for my arms. They were constantly afraid I would fall and injure myself more. Maggie had to send them out of the room when she came to see me now, just so they would let me do things on my own. She was due in soon and Damian was pacing the room, waiting for her to arrive. The meeting between Fennik, Niklaus and King Harold didn't go well. He assumed they were just telling tales until this morning. Valyn got the call from his father during a rather intimate moment, and he had to leave. I wasn't thrilled about that, but he promised we'd continue later. He went and got Damian to come sit with me while he found his other brothers.

"You're going to walk a hole in the carpet if you keep pacing around on the same spot." I giggled at him. He stopped his pacing and glanced at me. His crimson eyes lighting up as his gaze met mine.

"Sorry, I just can't be late for this meeting. As much as he didn't want to take the threat serious a week ago, things have changed now. I don't know what this will mean for any of us." He sat down in the chair by the fireplace and put his head in his hands.

"Then go. Maggie knows where I am, and Lydia can help me if I need it." I learned a few days ago that Lydia was the head maid in the home and the in-home healer for the Princes and now for me as well.

"I said I can't be late. I didn't say I want to leave you." His phone rang in his pocket. He pulled it out and held it up to his ear and I could hear the female voice on the other end yelling at him before he even spoke a word to him. He rolled his eyes. "Are you just going to scream at me or let me speak?" His words were clipped and short, the irritation in his voice was very obvious. More words came through the phone, none of which I could make out. At last, he spoke, and his words were cold. "I have no time for this bullshit or drama. Bastian and I won't be at the White Oak anymore. Get over it." He hung up the phone, and I quickly looked away. I think I wasn't supposed to hear that.

He got up and came over to the bed, sitting down beside me. "Maggie should be here shortly. You don't have to wait." I leaned my head on his shoulder, his head resting back on mine.

"I shouldn't have answered that call. If someone named Rita shows up here, she is not welcome. Garth will remove her from the property." He sighed, and I didn't understand why he was telling me this.

"Who is she?" I asked, not sure if I wanted to know.

"A fling that Bastian and I used to share when we were drunk or high to escape our lives. She wanted more from us, but we had no interest. Some idiot gave her our numbers, and she's been harassing us since. We no longer go to her place of employment and the owner has been salty since." He lifted his head and looked down at me. I knew they had lovers before me, but why did hearing that chip away at my heart? "It's over Luna. Bastian and I haven't gotten high since the night you got attacked. I may have had a few drinks to keep myself here that night and not go back to the Mor and sleep outside of your door, but that's been it."

"Your hundreds of years older than me. I can't expect me to be your first fling, right?" The words were hard to get out like I couldn't breathe. *Fling.* Was that what this was? Niklaus said that when I first met him, they would tire of me. Maybe they would and they would replace me like Rita. My heart started racing, but Damian grabbed my face between his hands and forced me to look up at him.

"Never associate you and the word fling together ever again. Is that understood?" His eyes became dark, his voice a command on my heart. I nodded my head, trying not to let the tears that threatened to escape fall down my face. "You are not a fling to me, or Bastian or even Valyn. As shocking as this comes to us, we can't lose you. The thought of this meeting and being away from you for even a day has the three of us on edge. We would bring you with us if we thought our father wouldn't take one look at you and try to keep you in his mountain villa as a prize."

"I highly doubt your father would do that." I whispered. My heart started humming as a presence entered the room.

"You don't know how our father works," Bastian's voice danced into the room and all around me. He smiled and came towards the bed. "No worries, little Luna. We won't let him have you."

Valyn entered the room a moment later. A vibration hit the room with us all in it. "Have you ever wondered why none of us look alike?" He asked as he took the seat at the foot of the bed.

"Not really. I don't look like my siblings at all." They looked at each other and back at me with a puzzled look on their faces. "Luther has light brown hair and blue eyes and Lily has mousey brown hair with light grey eyes. Then there is me, blue hair that I try to dye blonde with dark brown eyes." I shrugged my shoulders.

"Our father has five mates, very rare, if we're being honest. Each mate had a son, the five of us. You could say that out of us all that Damian and I are the closest. Our mothers are sisters. I grew up thinking it was weird but honestly," Bastian said as he gazed at me, then to his brothers. "I get it now."

Maggie entered the room just as Damian was about to speak. "Okay boys, get out. You have a meeting and her and I have business to attend to." They each smiled at me, each giving me a quick kiss on the cheek before heading towards the door.

"We will see you tonight Luna. Get dressed for a nice dinner, we're going out," Valyn said, grinning from ear to ear. I couldn't hide my smile. Maggie closed the door behind them and turned to me with a cheshire smile.

"Oh, we must definitely talk." Maggie walked back over to me and handed me another red vial of sweet liquid. I took it and downed it in one gulp. "Should I add a monthly aid tonic for you as well?" I almost spit the medicine out onto the bed. She wasn't joking, but it didn't take away the anxiety I had. I was worried that she would judge me when it came to them or scold me, but she never did.

"Yes, please. Do you think I'll be able to get more walking in today?" I asked her, wanting to rush past the topic.

"We are going to have you try running today. You've been doing well with walking. Now it's time to get that strength back." She smiled and helped me ease out of bed. I can't wait to feel the wind on my face again. I got dressed as fast as my body would let me and we headed out to the back courtyard. I saw Lydia and Garth on my way out. Both smiled at me. I waved in return. Garth, being the head of the castle guard, was always around. He was really nice, and I think he has a thing for Lydia. I'll have to talk to her about that later. As we got closer to the courtyard doors, the delectable scent of something sweet swirled around me. My smile grew wider as the smell of apples and cinnamon reached me. This place was becoming more like my home with each passing day.

CHAPTER 31
VALYN

The mountain villa was always much colder than I preferred. The wind whistled through the trees as we walked up to the front doors. The engraved the large oak doors had intricate vine work and what looked like blood lilies and sapphire blooms around the edges. Niklaus was ahead of us, murmuring about something. I think he is still pissy that Luna is at the house and that our father refused to do anything about it.

The large front doors opened up as we got closer. I noticed Xavier and Maddox standing on guard. I nodded to both men as we entered. The huge, cavernous room was nice and warm. The fireplace at the back of the room had a roaring fire bringing life to the space. Athena, the head maid of the house, smiled at us in greeting.

"It's good to see you boys. Your father is right this way." Her auburn curly hair bounced as she turned on her heels and lead us towards the dining hall. She was older than us by a good two hundred years, but she acted as if she was a teenager from this day and age. She looked back over her shoulder. "I hope you boys are hungry. Your father has a guest and there is food a plenty."

"If Dudley did the cooking, I will definitely be eating," Bastian said, rubbing his stomach. When wasn't he hungry? Athena chuckled and looked back down the hall.

"You said Father has a guest. Would this guest be the reason he summoned us?" Nik asked and Athena just shrugged her shoulders. She played house maid well, but her family is the best assassins and spies that our continent has seen. She knows a great deal more than she should, but she is loyal to our father and Nik should've known that she wouldn't answer him.

She came to a halt in front of the open doorway. "Right this way, your highnesses." She bowed at the waist as we passed her single file, youngest to oldest as father always preferred.

The dining hall was a large room with a massive table in the middle. The doors to the courtyard were closed today, thankfully, but the fireplace was lively. At the head of the table sat our father, the man of ever-changing looks. The broad shoulders, short dark colored hair that looked like the galaxy itself, and the deep grey eyes made up the mountain of a man sitting in the chair. He cut his hair shorter than usual, and he looked as if he was about to break the chalice in his hand. "Sit, we have much to talk about."

One by one, we filled our usual seats, Fennik and Nik on the left of our father and Bastian, Damian and me on the right. We looked at the other end of the table, at the other huge male. His bright blue and grey hair was shorter than I remembered, but his honey gold eyes remained the same. Lord Drake, the Lord of Mirith and the King of Hildaria, sat across from our father. I bowed my head in acknowledgement towards the Lord. Why he didn't use the King's title was beyond me, but who was I to question?

"Lord Drake was just informing me about the matter of a war that is being threatened on his lands. Fennik and Niklaus had come to me prior to this meeting asking me questions about the royal legions starting a war, and I told them to stop spreading baseless rumors. Until you showed up this morning telling me the same things, my sons spoke of." He looked at my brothers as if accusing them of going behind his back.

"My son, Prince Nox, came to me a few days ago with news that General Rothsberg is gathering the beast and dragon legions to raid Hildaria. I would've been here sooner, but I had to see to some protection matters back home just in case an attack happens in my absence. I trust you would do the same if you were in my position." Lord Drake was usually a very carefree person, very kind, but calculated.

"I would, but I also appreciate you coming and requesting to speak to me personally about the matter. I have not made an order to attack your kingdom. It wouldn't be wise seeing as our people have been allies for centuries. An attack on you would trickle into Mistveil and our people would be hurt as well." My father loosened his grip on his chalice and sat back in his seat.

"I am curious, King Harold," Lord Drake sat forward, putting his elbows on the table, resting his chin on his now folded hands. "How did your sons come of this information?"

Our father waved towards Fennik to speak, and he relayed the entire information that he got from Luna. Lord Drake stilled in his chair at her name. He looked over at the three of us and back at our father. "Is she here?" it came out as a quick question. Why was he asking about her?

"She is currently at the castle. She was injured in a borg attack and has been healing under the care of the high priestess. With whom she is currently with." I spoke up, trying to keep my tone in check.

"I would like to go visit her when we are done. I haven't seen her since she was a child." He smiled and something felt different. A shift in the air had Damian, Bastian, and me staring at Lord Drake. A piece of the puzzle finally clicked into place.

"Feel free to take her with you. It's not like we want her here." Niklaus snipped from the other end of the table. Before I could say anything, a sharp smack sounded through the room. We all flinched. Our father had just backhanded Nik as if he was a child who spoke out of line.

"Lord Drake, my apologies. My son doesn't know when to keep him mouth shut when it comes to his own personal feelings." Lord Drake shook his head and waved it off.

"It is fine. As much as I would love to have Luna come stay with me back in Mirith. As of now, it is unsafe for her. However, once Nox is done with his duty at Lithstrum I would like for him to come and visit. He hasn't seen Luna in a bit, and I think it would be good for them to catch up." Lord Drake looked at us and I couldn't tell if it was in warning or acceptance.

"We would love to have your son here. Is he not riding with dragon legion then?" Our father picked at the meat on his plate.

"No, he was supposed to ride with General Gunther's son, but seeing as my son rather drop him into a volcano or the Kilspur ocean, it's for the best." He shrugged and sipped from his glass of what smelled like spiced rum.

"Oh? Captain Luther Cromwell comes highly recommended, if I am not mistaken. I'm surprised your son wouldn't find it an honor to ride with his former rider's son." Luther, that was Luna's brother. Maybe Prince Nox saw Luther around Luna and didn't like what he saw.

"Well, if you all can keep a secret, I will fill you in." We all nodded, and he continued, "Please do not let Luna find out. It would hurt her if she knew. If you don't know already, Luther is Lunas older brother. She asked Nox to please keep a friend of hers safe, sadly Luther attacked my son and her friend, Captain Virgil Crawley, witnessed the incident and grabbed Luther off of my son and in the process Luther's knife went from my son's throat into Virgil's chest. Thankfully, Nox was able to get Virgil to Lithstrum, but it will take more time before he can fully recover. Virgil is the friend that Luna asked him to keep safe and my son is repaying not just a life debt but also a promise." He brought the glass back up to his lips and downed the liquid in one smooth gulp. Damian froze at the name, Bastian looked at him, and he nodded. Is this man someone we should worry about? "I believe this attack in your name is an act of treason from the humans in a retaliation."

"For what?" My father's question was pointed and direct. He wouldn't assume treason right away, but there could be plenty of reasons the humans would try to revolt against us. He used them as disposable pawns every time he went to war.

"I'd suggest talking to the General yourself. Ask him about it." He handed me a photo. "Please pass that down if you would." I took the photo and handed it down the line, each of us looking at the photo. Hordes of beasts lined the Mitos mountains on Hildaria's' side.

My father took the photo from Damian who was a ghost white. "Is this the full beast legion?" He looked at Damian, who just shook his head. "What would you say the percentage is?"

"At least a third of the beast legion is there. If they are acting on orders claiming that you willed this, that will cause a big issue for us. I'll head over to where the camps look set up immediately and find Commander Ilsum, I don't know why he wouldn't come to me first." Damian said. "May I be excused?"

"In a moment, the three of you take Lord Drake to go see your friend. Fennik and Niklaus, you two will go with Lord Drake back to Mirith when he is done. Meet with the armies there and then go get General Cromwell. We need to have a meeting." With a wave of his hand, we stood. Lord Drake nodded his head towards our father.

"Harold, I know this isn't you. No one else besides Nox and your sons knows about that photo. But if it got out, you're up here in your mountain villa in the Mito's." He shook his head. "The legions are closer to your back door than you realize, and that won't look well to outsiders. Be safe, my friend." With that, Lord Drake stood and looked at us. "Shall we then?" He turned on his heels and walked out the door. The three of us bowed to our father and followed the lord out of the villa. I wonder what Luna is doing now.

CHAPTER 32
LUNA

I was dripping sweat. Running laps around the large fountain in the courtyard was a lot harder than just walking around it. I pushed myself harder than I have the last few days. Maggie whistled, and I slowed my pace.

"Come get some water before you pass out." She waved me over to where she was sitting on a small stone bench. I lightly jogged to her and sat down. "You're recovering much quicker than I expected you to. This is a pleasant surprise." She poured me a glass of water, ice clinking in the glass. I took the glass and drank deeply. The water here tasted so much better than back home. Everything tasted better here.

"Do you think I'll be good to go for a walk around the city with the princes later?" I asked between swigs of water.

"As long as you let them help you if you start hurting. You're doing well, but I don't want you to push yourself." She patted me on my knee and stood up. "It's getting late, go get cleaned up. I asked Lydia to get you a dress for tonight. Flats though, no heels. Not yet anyway.

Knowing those three, you'll be out most of the night. There is also a tonic in your room on the night table."

I stood up and hugged her. "I don't think I have said this yet but thank you. You've been really kind to me and haven't judged me once. I really appreciate it."

"Luna, I have a question for you." She asked me, halting me before I walked away. I nodded at her to go on. "Have you ever heard the words mate or mating bond?" "They mentioned something about it this morning. About how their fathers mated to each of their mothers and how rare it is. But that's about it." I said, trying to think if they said anything else.

"Yes, mates are a very rare thing. King Harold has five now, rare as it is, it isn't completely unheard of. I explained to Damian a little while back my theory on why that is." She sat back down, and I sat down next to her. "My mate was human. King Harold had a set of challenges he gave to him. He gives these challenges to any humans who have little to no fae heritage, who fall for a fae or a fae falls for. My husband took the challenges, and King Harold gave him an immortal fae life. Losing a mate can cripple or even kill the one still alive. Hence why he keeps his mates in the mountain villa with him, safe and protected. He lost his very first mate before Damian was born, and it wrecked him. She was pregnant with child."

"So, Damian isn't the oldest? Do they know there was another sibling?" I asked, afraid to know the answer.

"No, we aren't allowed to talk about them. I'm only telling you because I see the look in their eyes when they see you. The look in your eyes. I could just be seeing things, but I believe you might be their mate." She whispered the last part.

"Me? But I'm human. They would've never met me if I didn't get injured. Would we even know?" The amount of questions running through my head was startling.

"They might have figured it out by now. It starts as a humming of the heart, like a vibrational pull. You think about them when you're not around them. You panic when you don't hear from them for long periods of time. But the love is unconditional and comes out of nowhere." She smiled at me. "If I am right about you, you are special, and those boys will let nothing happen to you." She patted my knee once more. "Enough talk. Go get cleaned up and dressed. Lydia will do your hair and makeup when you're done."

I walked out of the courtyard and into the castle. I pulled my shoes off at the door and carried them back to my room. My head was spinning. There was no way I could be their mate. We just met. They barely know me, and I barely know them. How in the world would do I talk to them about this? What if I'm not good enough for them? These thoughts kept swirling in my head as I walked down the hall to my room. I will talk to them tonight. It was the only chance I'll probably have. I took a deep breath when I got to my door. I reached for the handle and pulled.

As soon as I opened up the door to my room, a soft pull tugged on my heart. My head snapped up and sitting in my room, each in their own chair, was the princes. I tossed my shoes to the side and closed the door behind me.

"Luna, we aren't alone." Valyn said as he stood and walked over to me. "You're requested on the patio." He kissed me on the cheek. I looked at Bastian and Damian. Both were paler than usual.

"Is something wrong?" I asked them all. Bastian stood and grabbed my hands.

"Go to the patio. We will be here when you get back." He kissed me quickly and handed me off to Damian, whose eyes were far away. I leaned down and kissed his cheek. His eyes moved to mine and I could see fear there. I didn't like that.

I pulled back and walked towards the patio, opening the doors. A familiar scent of mint and fresh rain coming off the mountain winds swirled around me. I walked out onto the patio and saw Lord Drake standing there, looking over Wardveil.

"Lord Drake! It's so good to see you again." I practically ran to the male before me. He opened his arms and awaited my usual hug.

"Its good to see you too, Luna." He smiled down at me and returned my hug, a tight embrace. "I was visiting King Harold and heard from his youngest that you were here. So here I am to visit my favorite person."

I let go and stepped back, smiling back at the Lord. "I have a question." He gazed at me and nodded for me to continue. "Did my mother ever make it to Mirith? She left ten years ago to come see you about a healer to help save my sister. We never heard from her again." I looked down at my hands, fidgeting like always. "Luckily, Lilly got help from Maggie, courtesy of Damian being a delivery man. She's the high priestess here. Sadly, my father didn't make it." Telling Lord Drake everything just spilled out like vomit. "I'm sorry, I shouldn't put a damper on our meeting."

"You're okay Luna. I have seen your mother. Please know she never abandoned you or your siblings. I cannot tell her story for her, but maybe soon you can come to Mirith yourself and see her." My eyes lit up. She was still alive! "I'm sorry about your father. But I'm glad Lilly is doing well. I won't be able to spend too much time here, but maybe once things settle you can come visit again." He hugged me again. I always saw Lord Drake as part of my family. He was so kind to me and always treated me like I was his own kid. I think that's why my father disliked him so much, but for years, this man practically raised me. I practically saw him as a second father.

"I would like that very much. Will you tell her I said hello and I love and miss her?" I asked him, happy tears streaming down my cheeks.

"Of course I will, princess." I hugged him tighter. I missed him. A part of me felt at home with him. "Sadly, I have to leave and head back home. Maybe the princes can escort you to Mirith soon. Are you planning on returning to Celvenia?" I thought for a moment.

"No, I don't think so. Once Lilly is better, she will move into the cottage in Wardveil with Harper and Kira. They decided it would be best to get out of the house where our father died. As far as Luther goes, I'm good. I love my brother, but if I go back home, he won't let me out of his sight again. He's overbearing, and I don't want to be controlled." I paused for a moment and looked back at the open doors and smiled. "The princes offered for me to stay here with them. Either here in the castle or find a place of my own. I think I'll take them up on that offer."

"I think that's a good choice. Just stay close to those three." He smiled at me once more, then said, "let's get you inside before they rush out here to check on you." He laughed and put his arm around my shoulder. "I missed you, kiddo." I wrapped my arms around his waist and squeezed.

"I missed you too, old man." He laughed deeper this time. We walked back into the bedroom and the Princes were sitting around the little table.

"No need to move. I'm just returning her to you all. I can see myself out, boys." He hugged me one last time and each of the princes watched intensely. They rose and bowed at Lord Drake as he left, closing the door behind him.

CHAPTER 33
BASTIAN

She looked thrilled when she came inside with Lord Drake. He seemed happy as well. She wasn't kidding when she said she knew him, but she failed to mention the now huge elephant in the room. She came over and sat on Damian's lap, grabbing his face and making him look at her.

"Okay, spill it grumpy." She held onto him until he looked her in the eyes. He sighed and kissed her.

"I have to go away for a little while. There is something I need to take care of with my legion. I need to make sure that someone else isn't making calls on my behalf." He put his arms around her waist and pulled her closer to him. Valyn stood up and walked over to the patio doors. I followed him, getting the hint.

"Let's give them some privacy. We don't know how long he will be gone." Valyn whispered as he pulled opened the doors and walked outside. I looked back at Luna and Damian. My heart hurt to see the sadness on their faces. Being away from her is going to hurt him more that I even want to think about. I followed Valyn outside and closed the doors behind me.

"I really hope Damian isn't gone too long. If it's more than a day or two, I think she'll end up forcing us to go find him." I chuckled as I took one of the seat by the railing. Valyn sat next to me.

"Can I ask you something?" He asked and looked at me with a serious look on his face.

"Sure, something tells me we're probably wondering the same thing, honestly." I said, leaning back in the chair looking out at the mountains.

"Probably, do you think she is our mate?" He was serious, which for Valyn was new. His whole demeanor was different since he had laid eyes on Luna. Hell, we all were different.

"I do. Damian, you and I all look at her the same way. And when we were taking her, her eyes flashed with a swirl of gold. I don't know if you saw it, but I did, and it just felt so damn right. Do you get that ethereal wind scent with her as well?" I asked, looking over at him.

"Yeah, I thought it was just something around her I was picking up, but if you smell it too, then maybe there is more to her than we know." Valyn sighed and looked back at the door. "Is it wrong that I want to barge in there and throw her back on the bed?" He chuckled.

"Nope, because I'm thinking the same thing. I think we should just let them have at it by themselves though. As jealous as I am that he's in there with her alone, he deserves it." I said, resting my head back on the chair and closing my eyes. The birds sung to one another in the trees off in the distance. I wonder if birds had mates like we do. Can they feel if their mate dies? I wonder if Damian feels it, too.

"Why did you and Damian give each other a look when they Lord Drake brought up this Virgil dude?" Valyn snapped my attention back to him.

"Luna wrote a letter to him when she got here. We thought maybe he was someone she was with. Something tells me he didn't get that letter. Not after what Lord Drake said." I couldn't help but wonder if him not getting that letter would cause us issues when he saw her again.

"Great. Well, when he sees her next, if he touches her or tries to touch her, I can't guarantee I won't take his hands off personally." Valyn flashed me a wicked grin and I couldn't help but grin as well.

"If he hurts her, he is dead. She may hate us for it, but that's a risk I'm willing to take. With everything she said about her first time, I don't like him, and I don't even know him." My thoughts wandered back to her, asking us not to leave her. The fear in her was palpable and I never want her to worry about us leaving her.

"Hey, don't forget, we still owe her a night out tonight. And after everything we just talked about, we need to make it a very good night." Valyn nudged my arm, and I smiled. We did indeed owe her a night out.

CHAPTER 34
LUNA

"I didn't know you had a legion of your own." I said to him, still sitting in his lap cuddled up to his chest. I honestly knew very little about the princes other than they were royalty, fae and extremely hot.

"I command the beast legions with Bastian. It looks like my legion, however, is the one at the forefront of the bullshit, and I don't appreciate finding it out from someone who isn't a part of my command." He hugged me closer to him, breathing into my hair. "I don't want to leave you, but I am not taking you with me. They might be my men, but I would not trust them around you. You would walk into the camp, and I'd have to kill half of them just for looking at you. I can't have that now, can I?"

I hugged him back and kissed his neck. He shuddered under my lips, and I decided he needed a quick distraction before he left me. I nipped at his neck gently as his hands tightened on my hips.

"What do you think you're doing?" He said playfully, glaring down at me. I bit my lower lip under his stare. My core beginning to turn molten under that stare.

"Nothing," I drawled out, returning his playfulness. It's time to show him what I've been working on. I stood up and pulled off my clothes, flinging them towards the basket in the room's corner. I needed a shower badly, two birds, one stone. Damian's eyes widened as he took in my ass in my tight pink underwear and sports bra that was barely keeping my breasts from spilling over the top.

"Have I ever told you how stunning you look like that?" Damian licked his lips and devoured me with his eyes as he adjusted himself. I pulled the hair tie out of my hair and put it around my wrist, running my fingers through my tangled ponytail. I turned away from him, letting my hair flow down my spine, and walked into the bathroom. I walked over to the shower, turning it on nice and hot. Damian practically fell out of the chair, trying to keep his eyes on me. I pulled off my bra, releasing my breasts from the tight fabric cage I forced them into earlier, and chucked it out the door. Before I could reach down to take off my underwear, Damian was in the bathroom behind me, grabbing at them.

"Don't rip them. I'm fond of these." I smiled and commanded at him. I don't know who picked these out, but the soft cotton fabric was a nice relief to the silky and lace underwear that took up a majority of the drawer.

"I won't rip them off if you don't fight me to get them off." He smiled and lowered himself down onto a knee. I watched him intently as he pulled them down with his teeth in one fluid motion. His eyes never leaving my own. He kissed back up my thigh and nipped into my hip with his teeth. I jumped at the slight burst of pain, and he grinned at me, raising up to his feet. He kissed me passionately.

The steam from the shower fogged up the mirror. He pulled out of the kiss and undid the buckle on his pants, letting them drop to the floor. I grabbed at his shirt and pulled it over his head, running my hands up his chest and down his arms. His boxers were all that was stopping me from the glorious sight of him. He looked down and tugged on the waistband, smiling at me. A dare.

I pushed him up against the wall and kissed him deeply. His lips parted, allowing me in. I ran my hand down his chiseled abs, down to the deep V at his waist, and into his boxers. I could feel his length press against my palm, and I was ready to take him. My fingers touched the silky, hard skin of his member. He moaned at the featherlight touch. I pulled my hand out of his boxers and pulled the waistband down around his hips and ass, letting them drop to the floor. His hard, thick length was at full, glorious attention. I dropped to my knees and opened my mouth, slowly taking him. The salty, sweet taste of him was amazing. I took him in almost fully to his balls, his head reaching the back of my throat. I pulled back slowly, running my tongue up the thickness of him, letting my tongue swirl around his glistening head. He grabbed me gently by the hair and pulled me up onto my feet to look me directly in the eye.

"That was a tease," he said, pulling my head to the side. He placed a kiss at the base of my neck. "I hope you're ready." He bit into my neck and sent a shock of pleasure and pain through me. My core throbbed as the intense heat flooded my body. He pulled back. A small trail of my blood dripped into his beard. He turned me around, bending me over the sink. "Now little Luna," He bent over behind me and whispered in my ear. "You're all mine." He lined his head up to my entrance and pushed in. I let out a little yelp at the sudden rush of pleasure. There was no promise of being gentle. This was pure raw passion and need. I pushed back against him, grinding myself on his thickness. The rush was intense. He pumped into me faster and harder, pulling me through a wave of release, but he wasn't done with me just yet. He pulled my hair, my head leaning back as he put his hand gently around my throat like a necklace. He kissed my head and whispered, "May I?" I throbbed around his length, and he squeezed at my throat. The feeling was magnificent, a whole new level of pleasure I didn't know existed.

With one hand on my throat and the other on my waist, I was about to come undone again on him. I didn't want to come alone; I matched his movements with my own, pushing back into him until he was fully sheathed in me. I gripped the sink tighter, a moan escaping me. He grabbed both my hips and thrusted harder into me; he growled and my core tightened on him. His release barreled into me as my release coated him in return. We stood connected for a minute longer before he pulled out of me. I whined and wiggled my ass, wanting him to stay put.

"Good thing the water's running." He slapped my ass, smiled and pulled me into the shower with him, kissing me once more. We let the water flow over us before he pushed me against the wall and took me again.

CHAPTER 35
LUNA

Damian got out of the shower first and dried off, grabbing a fresh, clean towel for me from the cabinet in the bathroom. He put the fluffy white towel around me and helped me step out of the shower. My legs were still shaking and slightly stinging.

"Come on, let's get you dried off and dressed. They better still take you out tonight." Damian said as we walked out of the bathroom. Bastian and Valyn were laying on the bed smiling at us.

"Don't worry, Damian, we are still taking her out tonight. You just worry about coming home to our girl." Bastian winked at me, eyes watching my every move.

"Here, put this on. Maggie said no heels, so sandals it is." Valyn got up off the bed and brought over a teal-colored short dress. He handed me a small light blue box with a silver ribbon tied to it. I grabbed it from him with a very puzzled look on my face.

"Just open it. It's a gift from me to you," Valyn beamed. I pulled off the silver ribbon and opened it up. I pulled out what I assumed to be a two-piece gold bikini that looked like it would barely cover my breasts and would be wedged up my ass all night. I glared at him. "What? We are going out tonight and you might have a need for that where we're going."

I dropped my towel to the floor and let them gaze at me. I walked over to Damian and pulled the towel from around his waist. I flipped it up over my head and gently wrung the water out of my hair. I was truly taking my time letting them watch me. I grabbed the scrap of gold fabric that was supposed to be the bottom and pulled it up slowly over my still pale legs. Gods, I needed a tan. I looked at myself in the full body mirror and smirked. I wasn't thin like most girls; I was curvy and thick, my thighs slightly touched, and I didn't always like what I saw in the mirror, but today, I glowed. I used to be self-conscious about my body, but these three made a lot of my insecurities vanish. I grabbed the top part of the bikini and tried to get it on by myself. Luckily, Valyn didn't want me to struggle. He came up behind me, still facing the mirror, and tied the top around my ribs and my neck. "Is this too tight?" He asked.

"No, it's perfect." I grabbed the sandals and put them on my feet, lacing them up my calves. They were a gorgeous cream color that could complement the dress perfectly. I stared at myself once more before reaching for the dress. It was a halter dress that buttoned once behind my neck and cinched at the waist, flaring out below. It was probably the most beautiful dress I had ever worn. I grabbed my brush from the bathroom and quickly ran it through my hair, pulling it to one side. My natural curls laid perfectly on my shoulder. I looked through my makeup bag and found a black eyeliner pencil, a tube of black mascara, and some red lipstick. Perfect. I know Lydia was supposed to do it for me, but I didn't want to wait. I quickly did my make up then returned to the main room to see their reactions. They all stared at me and I second guessed my decision to do it myself.

"You are the most beautiful creature I have ever seen." Valyn said. I could feel my cheeks heating.

"So where exactly are going?" I asked, out of curiosity.

"We're heading to the summer realm. It's Valyn's home outside of the castle." Bastian said. He smiled at me and got off the bed to hug me.

"Your realm?" A confused look took over my face as I glanced over at Valyn.

"We each are princes of a different realm, seasonal and solar. I am the Prince of Summer. Bastian is the Prince of Winter, Fennik is the Prince of Autumn, Niklaus is the Prince of Spring-" Valyn was cut off.

"Then there is me. I am the sole Prince of the solar and lunar realms." Damian kissed me on the cheek. I had no idea when he got dressed and I was slightly upset that he had clothes on. "I have to go. Maybe when I get back, we can go to one of my realms."

I put my arms around Damian's waist and put my head on his chest. "I would really like that." He put his finger under my chin and raised my head. He kissed me so passionately. I was sad when he pulled away, but he placed me in Bastian's arms.

"Take care of her guys." He turned away and headed for the door. He whispered something under his breath, but I couldn't hear him.

Bastian leaned down and kissed my cheek. "He will be okay. Don't worry about him. He's tough, and it's not like he's going off to battle. It's just a meeting. Now, let's go get you dinner." He took my hand and walked me into the hallway.

Valyn closed the door behind us and put his arm around me. "You've never been to my rooms before. Let's fix that." We got to the end of the hallway, and they led me up the main stairwell and down the hall. Valyn put his hand over my eyes. "This is going to be a surprise."

I heard a door open, and the smell of the sea and the sound of gulls were all around me. "Welcome to the Summer Realm." Valyn said in my ear, removing his hand from the eyes.

CHAPTER 36
LUNA

My eyes adjusted as light from the fading sun flooded off of the ocean before me. The air was balmy, a cool breeze whispered through the palm trees and across the sand. I took a step towards the beach, waiting for a hand to stop me that never came. They didn't try to stop me, so I took another step. It was beautiful. The clear blue water, peppered with little boats off the shore, looked like it went on for miles. The pinkish blue sky was fading to a deep royal blue, the sun setting behind the mountains on a far-off island. I walked onto the sand and looked out at the water; it called to me like a song on the wind. A large hand wrapped around my waist, pulling me into the arms of the fae Prince of Summer, Valyn. Something settled deep in me at the touch of him here in his home. It's like a song that found its harmony was singing around us.

"What do you think?" He asked, holding me tightly, looking out at the water with me.

"I feel like the word beautiful just doesn't describe what I feel properly. It's absolutely stunning here." I looked up as the stars began winking into existence in the distance. Light footsteps came up behind us in the sand. I didn't need to look to know it was Bastian. He slipped his hand into mine, entwining our fingers together.

"Let's go get something to eat. I bet you haven't eaten at all today." Bastian said. As if it had a mind of its own, my stomach growled in response. Both males laughed a deep belly laugh and turned me away from the water and back to the sprawling town. The streets were a pale tan cobblestone with tall palm trees and beautiful sandstone buildings lining the streets. Valyn reached down, grabbing my other hand. Hand in hand, we walked down the sidewalk towards the alluring smell of food. The music from the local bars and restaurants flooded the streets, swirling all around us.

"There are so many places here to eat, sleep, and see the sun rising and setting." Valyn spoke as I took in my surroundings. Was this what it felt like to be free? I never went out like this. My nights always revolved around cooking and taking care of my family, or Kira and Harper taking me to their shows. Virgil and I never went to dinner or even out for a walk together without Luther or Kira and Harper supervising us.

My feet stopped moving as the realization sunk in. I had never had a moment alone to explore back home. I was nothing more than a controlled woman who was never allowed to do what she wanted. I couldn't go to the market without Harper. I wasn't allowed in the art galleries or the museums. I could sell my art as long as I had supervision at the market. Virgil never wanted to be seen alone with me. It was like he didn't want people to see us together. I know I'm not the prettiest girl or the thinnest, but is that why he didn't want to be seen with me? My chest tightened and I couldn't breathe as my brain kept pointing out everything I couldn't do. Bastian stopped us and put his fingers beneath my chin and made me look at him.

"What's wrong?" He studied my face, but I didn't know how to answer him. I don't want to tell them I am thinking about someone else while I was with them. They would take it the wrong way. But what was I to them, anyway? I know Maggie thinks we're mates, but what if she's wrong?

They will bore of you and toss you aside. I tried to shake my head, but I couldn't.

The thought of what Niklaus said now felt like a weight on my chest, drowning me in my thoughts. Bastian gripped my cheeks and kissed me. The smell of pine and snow swirled around me, calming my breathing.

"Breathe Luna, take a deep breath and come back to us." Bastian pulled out of our kiss and looked down at me with panic in his eyes. Valyn squeezed my hand, letting me know he was still there. I took a deep breath and held it.

One.

Two.

Three.

I exhaled and looked at them both.

"What am I to you?" I choked out the words, but I needed to know. I didn't want to think I meant something to them just to have them cast me aside for someone else they meet at a bar. They looked at each other, contemplating how to respond. That alone made my stomach turn. I regretted asking them instantly. Bastian put his hand back in mine.

"Come on, we're going to get dinner, and we will talk there." Valyn pulled us towards a small little restaurant that had little outdoor seating but looked full. He walked us inside and requested a private table in the back. The hostess smiled at him and tried running her hand along his, but he pulled it away. She grabbed some menus and led us to the back of the establishment, sitting us far away from the others gathered in the room. Valyn smiled at everyone as we made our way to the table.

The table was a wraparound corner booth with a full view of the restaurant. The booth itself had nice blue plush padding, so the wood wouldn't be so hard on the backside. I slid into the middle of the booth, sliding my hands over the padding, with Valyn and Bastian taking up a spot on either side of me.

A redheaded young man came over to the table and asked if we were thirsty. "I want some wine, please. I don't care what kind, just wine." I blurted out. I was still having a full-blown anxiety attack in my mind. The fact they didn't answer me outside didn't help my mind from wandering to the worst possibilities. The boys ordered whiskey and looked at me.

"Okay, before we answer your question. A word of warning: fae wine differs from human wine. It will make you a drunken fool quicker than you can say sorry. So be careful drinking it." Bastian said, looking over the table at Valyn like this was a bad idea.

"I get it, take my time, eat, drink water. Gotcha." I looked across the room and saw the hostess still staring over at us. Goddess, was she going to be watching us all freaking night?!

Valyn drew my attention to him by rubbing his hand on my leg under the table. "This is going to be a tough conversation for us." He took a deep breath before continuing. "What you are to us..." He paused again, like this was the hardest thing for him to say. He took another deep breath. "No, what you are to me is something I can barely put into words. From the moment I laid eyes on you, something in my head started screaming at me to get close to you, get between you and my brothers. I literally wanted to punch them all. Slowly, over the short amount of time we've all been together, the screaming no longer comes when you're near Bastian or Damian.

Fennik and Niklaus are a totally different story. If they look at you the wrong way, I will probably stab them both. But my heart keeps beating with one word in mind: *mine*. You are mine. But that is not a choice I can make for you. And definitely not something I would force on you. I know what you are to me, but I also know you are that same thing to my brothers, too. At least to Bastian and Damian." Valyn spoke in a low tone, his hand making idle circles up and down my thigh. Bastian leaned closer to me and put his arm behind my back, running his fingers along my shoulders.

"Panic set in when I saw Damian screaming into the house after he brought you to the Mor. I have never seen him like that before. We hunted the borg down and killed it for hurting someone innocent. When I saw you laying in that bed, I had to force myself to sit at the end of the bed. Hindsight seemed like a perfect place since your eyes liked to take in the view." He smiled at me, my cheeks heating. "I couldn't help but stare at you. Your eyes and lips were like an invitation I wanted to take you up on. Clearly I did eventually but, in all seriousness. The thought of you being out of my sight and out of my arms is maddening. Being away from you those few hours in the mountains at the meeting drove me insane. I knew you were home with Maggie, and you were safe, but with none of us there, it didn't ease the roaring in my head to get back to you. I saw it there in your eyes, though. You, between the three of us, just felt right. The look in your eyes, that spark of light, matched the one in mine, the one I saw when Damian and Valyn looked at you. The word mine doesn't even describe what you are to me."

I looked between them and my heart sung like an answering chord, wanting to twine with theirs. Valyn looked at me. "What are we to you Luna?"

A simple question, but a world of fear behind it. They were being honest with me, and I owed it to them. "Mate." I whispered the word out into the world and the two of them stilled. The fear in my mind came back to the front, howling at me for saying it out loud.

"Say it again," Bastian choked out. The server walked back over with a bottle of red wine and a bottle of whiskey. He placed the glasses on the table. Valyn looked up at the boy. "Come back in five." The boy nodded and walked away. Valyn and Bastian looked at me. The intensity in their stare was hard to look away from.

"Mate," I whispered once more, looking down at my hands, beginning to fidget with them once more. My anxiety was at an all-time high and I worried I messed up. Bastian pulled my chin up to look at him. I tried to keep my gaze low. I couldn't look at the disappointment I knew was on his face. He ducked his head down to look me in the eye. They glowed a bright silver with a hint of gold, no hint of disappointment in them. He lifted my head once more and turned me to face Valyn, his turquoise eyes now a liquid baby blue with a swirl of gold around the pupil. My heart raced as they looked at me.

"Luna, none of us believed in mates. We didn't even think it would be a possibility for us. We have seen our father with all our mothers. The intensity of the bond. None of us truly remember or even know what it was like for them. But you, you have a vibration to you that our bodies and minds answer to. I for one believe now. You are my mate. If that means I have to share you with my brothers, then I will try my best to play nicely." Bastian winked at me and kissed me.

"Well shit, I thought I was going to be the intense one tonight. Luna, Damian believes you are his mate. It is not just us. I had a feeling when I couldn't think straight after meeting you. My thoughts lingered on you and those beautiful lips of yours. I accept you as my mate Luna. Just know that you have to deal with our asses from now on." He smiled at me. I looked over at the hostess, who perked up at seeing Bastian and me kiss. I grabbed Valyn by his beard and pulled him into a deep kiss. Bastian let out a low whistle.

Valyn kissed me back passionately. I broke the kiss and looked over at the hostess, who now had somewhere else to be. Good. They followed my line of sight and laughed. "Did you do that just to make someone jealous?" Bastian whispered.

I smiled sweetly at them, "Who me? No, never."

The young boy came back over to the table and took our order. Valyn popped the cork on my wine and let me drink.

CHAPTER 37
VALYN

If I knew the wine was going to hit her as hard as it did, I wouldn't have let her drink it at all. She ate, I'll give her that, but she forgot the part about drinking water, though. Any other drink we offered her besides wine she was refusing. We left the restaurant an hour ago, and she booked it straight for the water. Watching Bastian try to contain her has been probably one of the best things I've seen here in a long time. Mr. Winter was sweating his ass off here, but he made it work for her. Gods, mate. She was our freaking mate. I never thought about me having a mate. I never imagined that I would find the same love our father had but, Luna looked at us the same way our mothers looked at our father. The pure desire and, dare I say, love.

"Will you stop just standing there and come help me?!" Bastian barked at me as Luna pushed him into the water, laughing. Gods, she was having fun. Did she ever have fun like this with someone else? I shook that thought from my head as I walked towards them with a grin on my face.

"You're in for it now, little one." I said, charging at her. She sidestepped me and I fell face first into the water. The hell? I swiped out at her feet, but she danced away further into the water. Bastian tried coming up behind her, but she was too fast, spinning out of his reach. She baffled both of us. We were fast, but she was somehow faster.

"Is that all you guys got?" She hiccupped between words. It was cute, but you could tell she was getting drunker the more she danced in the sand.

"Little one, if you don't stand still, you'll fall and get hurt. We don't want that." I said to her as I picked myself up off the ground. She stuck her tongue out at me and turned on her heels and booked it. Dear gods, Maggie healed her alright.

Bastian bolted after her through the sand. I jumped into the water, shifting to my shark form. I was faster in the water than I was on land. Bastian took the hint and shifted into his wolf. We had to get to her before she got hurt. Note to self: fae wine and Luna means super-fast drunk fun Luna. Why couldn't she be happy, fun drunk Luna in bed instead?

She was beautiful. Her hair seemed more blue tonight under the moonlight. Honestly, come to think of it, the blonde in her hair has been fading more and more the longer she's been with us. Tonight, she glowed. A stunning gold lined her body as she ran. She looked so free and happy I felt bad trying to stop her. I looked ahead to where she was running. Shit!

Panic set in when I realized she was running straight for Fangs Lagoon. "BASTIAN GET HER NOW!" I shouted to him. He picked up the pace, but somehow she was faster. She undid the button on the top of her dress, letting it fall to the sand behind her. If I wasn't in a panic for her safety, I would definitely enjoy the view.

I kicked it into high gear, rushing for her. She spun around on her heels and blew us both a kiss and jumped straight into the Lagoon. Shit!

LUNA

The water was warm. I couldn't see much in front of me in the now dark water. A glimmer of pink and yellow flashed around me. I broke the surface and heard a splash sounding far off behind me. I laid on my back and stared up at the stars. They could catch up with me.

The wine was delicious, it still warmed my body. Floating like this made my head stop spinning. The weightlessness of my body in the water was the best feeling I could have alone. I wish Lilly was here. She would love it here. I hope she was okay. I truly hope that Kira and Harper get her out of there.

I heard something break the water's surface; I forced myself upright, moving my hands and feet gently to keep me a float. "Took you two long enough." I said, as I faced the splashing sound.

The two faces looking at me were beautiful, but not the males I was expecting.. Two tanned females, one with long pink wavy hair, the other with shorter bright yellow hair, smiled at me. I looked at where I thought the shore was and didn't see it. How far did I float? Panic took over.

"Don't worry, you're safe," the pink-haired woman said, looking at the other.

"You took a beautiful dive, darling. But didn't anyone tell you not to come to Fangs Lagoon?" The yellow-haired woman spoke. I shook my head no. I did not know that I wasn't supposed to be here.

"Do you know what we are?" The stories from my childhood started filling my head. Mermaids. Valyn said they were dangerous, but these two didn't look so bad.

"Mermaids?" I said. My head was a little foggy still. Great, I was meeting mermaids for the first time and I was drunk. Perfect first impression.

"Good. Then you know what we do to pretty little fae like you?" The pink haired one spoke, her voice sounding like an echo.

"I'm not fae." I declared. What in the world made them think I was a fae?

"Are you sure about that?" They giggled in unison. I was ready to head back to shore but, which way was that? I looked around but still didn't see the shore.

"Yes, human mother, human father. Bred a human girl." My head was spinning. I tried to swim away, but something tugged at my ankles.

"Oh no, you're not leaving. It's been so long since a fae with your abilities has ventured into our lagoon." I didn't know which one was speaking to me, but the hold on my ankles got tighter. "I hope you can hold your breath."

Before I could scream, they pulled me under the water. Panic set in. My mind started racing. The two beautiful women came into full view. Each had a beautiful woman's upper body with the lower body of what looked like a shark. They had nothing covering their ample breasts, leaving them bare for any to see.

They smiled wide at me, revealing their sharp fang like white teeth. I tried to swim to the surface but failed. The tightness around my ankles turned razor sharp, blood started rising around me. The yellow-haired woman swiped at me with her hands, her fingers like sharp claws. I dodged out of her reach, but barely. Her nails cut my arm, leeching more blood into the water. The other swiped at my legs. Using all my strength, I tried to push myself through the water. She missed my legs but struck whatever held my ankles.

They were circling me; I reached down and grabbed at what felt like a rope made of seaweed, just sharper. Pulling at it, tearing the flesh from my hands, I ripped my left ankle free. The pink-haired one lunged at me again, but I kicked at her this time. Catching her face with my heel. The other sprang at me. I quickly pulled my other leg high. She sliced clean through my last thorny chain. Freed at last, I hurried for the surface, breaking free to catch my breath. The shore was far, but at least I could see it now.

I swam as quick as I could, the two mermaids coming up faster behind me. Claws dug into my leg, and I screamed, kicking with my other leg to get free. My heel collided with what I would guess was a nose. My leg was in searing pain. I had to get to the shore soon before I lost too much blood. They grabbed at my legs once more, sinking their claws into me. A warmth flooded into my body, as a golden glow filled my eyes. Panic rushed into me, and I threw my hands out at the mermaids. The light was like a beacon of fire. The mermaids' beautiful, twisted faces set in pain as their bodies slowly disintegrated in the light.

The light slowly dimmed as I pushed myself closer to the shore. A large great white shark was swimming fast at me and I screamed. Valyn shifted quickly, grabbing me and holding me to him. His eyes were wide, but he yelled towards the shore, "I GOT HER!" Bastian shifted back just in time for me to see him before I passed out.

CHAPTER 38
DAMIAN

The chill air on the mountains cut through my bones. Campfires lined up in between tents, chattering and growls could be heard loud and clear the closer I got to the encampment. The black tents had the night realm crest on them, a crescent moon with a sapphire bloom in the middle. I didn't see any of the navy-blue tents that housed the winter realms legions here. Good, one less thing to deal with. The larger of the tents had a warm fire right outside the front. Commander Ilsum was definitely in there.

I walked between the tents, beast and riders alike, bowing as I went. I could deal without all of that. I walked right into the large open tent and, sure enough, Commander Ilsum was looking at a map on the table in front of him.

"This is a surprise." Commander Ilsum looked up from the map, his eyes going wide as I entered. "I wasn't aware that we were camping out in the Mitos. Care to explain?"

"What do you mean you weren't aware? Your highness, you were the one who sent us here." Commander Ilsum grabbed a letter off of the table next to the map and handed it to me. I looked at him puzzled but took the piece of paper.

Commander Ilsum,

Gather the mountain riders and have them along the northern part of the Mitos Mountains in three days' time. Await my orders on our next move. Keep it to just the mountain riders for now. Set up camp and wait. Do not make a move without my order.

-Prince Damian

I looked over the letter and looked at my commander. "You seriously think I would write this? In all the centuries that we have worked together side by side, when in the hell have I ever used my official title to sign any letter to you? Also, was it sealed with the usual wax crest?" I asked him, tossing the letter into the fire.

He shook his head. "No, it wasn't. Damian, I am so sorry. One of General Rothberg's men delivered the letter. I thought you were keeping things official since someone else was delivering the letter." He looked at the map again, then at me. "What is going on?"

"Someone with knowledge of our entire operation is making some play calls on our behalf, apparently. Celvenia is under order to gather the dragon rider's legion to the forefront in Hildaria. King Drake spotted you all here and came to visit us. I want the legion gone from here by nightfall. Is that understood? We will not go to war with one of our oldest allies." I said as I turned and looked out at the legion that was gathered. Roughly 500 men and beasts.

"That is good news. The people were worried about this fight. Not out of fear of losing, but out of fear of the amount of lives that would be lost on both sides." He came up beside me and put his hand on my shoulder. "Something is different about you. Normally, you would've bitten my head off and kicked my ass."

"There is something different. I'll tell you when I'm certain, though. As for now-" a howl came from the skies, lightning hit the ground in the center of the camp. We ran out of the tent and looked up just in time to see a large two-headed black and white dragon fly away.

"Was anyone hit?!" Commander Ilsum yelled out. Grunts and growls came, but no injuries.

"I want everyone off the mountain and back home to the dusk realm. There is someone trying to cause dissent in our ranks. Unless you hear it directly from me, assume it's false and report it to the Commander. Even if it comes from General Rothsberg." I spoke loud and clear, so there was no misunderstanding. "Stay alert and ready. Something tells me we will see battle, but not against Hildaria. GO!"

Everyone broke away and started packing up the tents, washing the fires out. "I'll have the portal ready now. Be safe, Damian. If war is coming and you're not ready," he shook his head.

"I'll be ready. Get word directly to Commander Flores. Bastian wouldn't bother with a letter, and he should know that, but just in case." Ilsum nodded his head in understanding.

A sharp pain shot through my chest, dropping me to my knees. Ilsum rushed to my side, "Are you okay?" He asked, worry lacing his words.

"Something's wrong. We have to hurry and get the portal ready and get everyone home." He helped me up to my feet, and I pulled a silver ring out of my pocket and slipped it on. The red garnet stone flashed, lighting up a doorway into the mountain itself.

The legion looked at me and nodded, message received. They rushed the doorway; it was large enough for at least two dragons to fly through comfortably side by side. As the last beast and rider ran through the portal, Ilsum looked at me.

"I'll be safe, just go!" He nodded and ran through the door right as it closed.

Rushing back down the mountains heading towards Mistveil was a blur. The pain in my chest was getting worse. I saw the castle in the distance and pushed harder. I shifted as I entered the back courtyard. A maid was cleaning up the living area. I slowed my pace as I came up behind her.

"Excuse me, do you know by chance where my brothers Damian and Valyn are?" I asked, trying not to startle her.

"Oh, good evening, sir. Your brothers, if I am correct, went to the Summer Realm for the evening. Can I do anything for you?" She smiled politely, waiting for my response.

"You've done enough. Thank you." I turned and headed up to the Summer Realm. Once out of sight from prying eyes, I booked it at full speed down to the entrance to the summer realm.

I flung the door open at the end of the hall; salty sea air stuck to my beard. The pain in my chest got more and more intense as I looked out over the beach. I saw a glowing golden light coming from the water and there, on the edge of the beach on the rocky outcropping, was Bastian, pulling something out of the water. Valyn pulled himself out of the water moments later and horror-struck me as I realized they pulled Luna out of the water. She wasn't moving. I took off in a sprint, heading directly for them. What the hell happened?!

CHAPTER 39
DAMIAN

It has been three days. Three days of Maggie yelling at us about Luna getting hurt again. Three days of worry and unease settling into my chest. Valyn was taking it the hardest. He blamed himself for letting her drink. Bastian blamed himself for not being fast enough to catch her. They replayed the story repeatedly as Maggie worked on her. They cut her up pretty badly. Bruises were forming around the scratches. The only thing that wasn't making sense was Valyn's recounting of the event in the water. He's been arguing with Maggie for the last twenty minutes about it.

"I'm telling you; she is fae! I saw the golden fire come out of her hands and shred those mermaids." Valyn was getting annoyed and needed to calm down before Maggie sent us all out of the room again.

"Even if she is, I am not doing any bloodwork without her consent. You will just have to deal with that. She may be your mate, but you don't have a say unless she tells me otherwise." Maggie said as she changed the bandages on Luna's legs.

"I didn't get to tell her. I wasn't there to tell her." I put my head in my hands. I wasn't there to save her. I wasn't there to tell her how I felt about her.

"I made sure she knew. You act like you won't be able to tell her your own self." Bastian put his hand on my shoulder and smiled down at me. "Stop sulking. If she wakes up and sees us all fighting or looking sad, she will be upset. Let's not have that."

Valyn turned his head to look at Bastian. "I'm sorry, is captain smartass being the level-headed one?" I had to agree. Usually, he was not the voice of reason. He just shrugged his shoulders.

A soft knock came at the door, and we all paused. Fennik entered the room looking as if he had seen a ghost. "The dragon legion attacked Mirith this morning. The castle is safe but, the town took a hit. They're flying the Mistveil banners." Fennik fell into the seat next to me.

"Where is Niklaus?" Valyn asked, now standing closer to Luna's bed. Bastian was flexing his fingers, opening, and closing them.

"He's still there. Him and Prince Nox have been at the forefront of the fight with one of our captains from Celvania." Fennik looked at us with pleading eyes. We looked between him and Luna lying on the bed. Seeing her lie in this bed constantly injured is becoming too much.

"Go. When she awakens, I will tell her where you are. I will also try to keep her here." Maggie knew why we had reserves. She honestly got it.

"I'll go to the mountain riders, Bastian, get to your legion. Valyn do you think you can get the naval unit ready and prepared to ride?" I stood up and walked to Luna.

"I'll get the naval unit ready from here and have them meet me. We have about six sea dragons and a few that can go between the air and sea. Where are the dragon legions camping and why in the hell aren't they listening to Prince Nox? He is the commander of them." Valyn pulled out his phone and walked out of the room.

"They're camped outside of the walls of Mirith. Prince Nox says there is someone controlling the dragons. They cannot shift into their fae forms. Captain Crawley thinks it is General Rothsberg." Fennik looked over at Luna. "What the hell happened while we were gone?"

"Too much has happened. We will have to fill you in later." Bastian was out the door a moment later, calling his own commander. This was going to be hard. I leaned down and kissed Luna on the cheek. "We will be right back." I whispered to her.

A soft whimper left her. A heartbeat later, Valyn and Bastian were standing next to me, staring at her. Maggie was on the other of her within seconds. Luna's eyes fluttered open. She looked up at us. Her normally dark brown eyes had a spiral of gold to them. The blonde in her hair had completely faded. Something was different about her.

"Don't sit up too fast." I urged her. She sat up gingerly and looked at Fennik.

"What's wrong?" Her voice sounded strained, like she had been screaming.

"That can wait. How are you feeling? You were asleep for a few days." Maggie asked her while checking her vitals again.

"I had the weirdest dream. I was swimming with mermaids, and they attacked me, but I lit them on fire, then poof. They were gone. It felt so real." Luna looked at Maggie and smiled. "I think I had too much wine last night. I don't even remember coming home."

Maggie looked at us all then back to her, "Luna, you've been home and asleep for the last three days. Your dream wasn't a dream." She checked Luna's temperature as she spoke. "The Princes yet again brought you back in a panic, covered in blood and unconscious. I've been changing your bandages and cleaning your wounds since. You don't remember any of it?"

Luna shook her head. "Wait, so if that was real." She paused. "The mermaids called me a fae. Last I checked, my parents were human, and I was human."

"What exactly did they say to you? Do you remember?" Maggie sat down on the edge of the bed and looked at Valyn. The apology in her eyes was enough. She didn't believe him earlier, and she felt bad about it.

"They said, *We haven't had a fae with your abilities here in a long time.* Maggie, I'm human. They must be wrong." Luna looked at each of us. Fennik's look of shock was written all over his face.

"The only way I can tell is if you allow me to do blood work. Valyn has been barking about you being fae and what he claimed to have seen in the water. I just didn't think it was possible. Usually, for a human to become a fae, they have to go through the descent. Which clearly you haven't." Maggie looked at Fennik. "Could you please get Lydia for me? I would ask these three, but they aren't about to leave her side anytime soon."

Fennik nodded his head and left the room in a hurry. If he didn't know or couldn't scent it before, he definitely could now. Luna smelled more like Valyn and Bastian. She accepted the bond with them and didn't reject it. Maybe she would accept the bond with me, too. I sat at the head of the bed and grabbed her hand.

"I'll sit with you while she does it. We do have to leave soon and head to Mirith. An attack happened this morning and we're needed. You just need to heal up. We won't be gone long." I kissed her cheek.

"Mirith was attacked?! Why?" she demanded, and I didn't understand the urgency or the need in her voice.

"That's what we need to find out." Bastian said from the foot of the bed. That was looking like his favorite place to be. Lydia and Fennik entered the room with a small metal cart full of needles and vials.

"I need you to sit completely still." Maggie nodded at Lydia, who put a strap around Luna's upper arm. Maggie grabbed a large needle and removed it from its sterile packaging. I let out a shudder. I have tattoos, but no thank you to those kinds of needles. They made my skin crawl. Luna nodded and looked at Bastian. He gazed back at her and then at me. I have a feeling he would've removed me from my spot if she asked. Maggie drew three vials of blood from her arm and released the strap from around her upper arm. "I will get these results back to you as soon as I get them. I'm not saying you need bed rest, just be careful. I know better than to attempt to stop you from going." She hugged Luna before she and Lydia left the room.

"No, you are not coming with us." Valyn was the one who spoke up and thank gods he did.

"I am going. Get over it." She threw back the blankets and stood up. Her nightgown was covering her up well. She stalked for the dresser, pulling out light blue jeans and a black tank top. She headed to the bathroom, slamming the door shut behind her. I walked over and knocked, hoping she would let me in. The lock clicked.

"Someone want to explain what's going on?" Fennik asked from the chair he took by the fireplace.

Well, the cat was going to get out of the bag somehow. "She's our mate," was all I needed to say for him to get up and walk to the door.

"Well, that definitely explains a lot." Fennik whistled.

The bathroom door opened a moment later, and she looked at Fennik. "Are you going to stop me from going?" She asked. Her words were flat and cold.

"Nope, I'm not. They might, but I won't. Clearly, there is something there you care about." Fennik inched closer to the door as if trying to escape before getting shot.

"Yeah." She paused and finally looked at us. "My mother's in Mirith."

CHAPTER 40
BASTIAN

"How do you know she's in Mirith?" I asked. Clearly, this is news to all of us. Valyn and Damian looked at her, then at me.

"When Lord Drake came here to see me, he confirmed she did indeed make it to Mirith, and that she didn't leave us. He wanted me to come visit so she could tell me what was going on." She looked out the window at the mountains. "I'm going with you to go see my mom. If you have a problem with that, too bad. I can find my way there on my own."

"Luna, it's a war zone. There is more going on there than we know." Valyn said, trying to step towards her. She moved back out of his reach.

"You act as if I don't know that. You realize Celvenia has had soldiers in the streets for years. That they would attack random people walking in the streets for fun. Accuse people of making comments about your father or Lord Drake, or even Ishtar himself. My father and Luther may have treated me poorly most of my life since my mom left, but one thing they taught me was how to hunt and fight. I can protect myself if that's what you're worried about." She was angry, but who was she angry at?

"Who are you really mad at Luna? I highly doubt it's anyone in this room." I said, not trying to sound like an asshole, but it was true.

"Whoever pulled the trigger on Mirith. My mother is there, I was born there. I won't let it fall. My life has been pretty meaningless up to this point. I am going. It's up to you if it's with or without you." She was cold. This wasn't the Luna we have grown to know for the last few weeks.

"You're not going." It was Fennik who spoke from the door. "At least not without any weapons. Let's go. I'll help you find something to use." He turned out the door. She looked at us, grabbed her boots and followed Fennik out the door.

"What the hell just happened?" I exclaimed. I couldn't think straight. My head kept yelling to follow her.

"Did you know anything about this?" Valyn asked me.

"I only knew that she was born in Mirith and that she said her mom went there to get help. I didn't know her mother was still alive." I replied, looking at the door.

"Let's go. If we try to stop her, I feel like Fennik will take her instead." Damian was already out of the room before either of us could reply. We followed him out of the room and down the hall to the far side of the castle. We had a good-sized armory, most just stuff we collected, but some stuff was passed down from our father.

As we made it to the armory, sure enough, the armory door was wide open and inside stood Fennik and Luna. She had Valyn's silver crossbow that's engraved with a wolf with sapphire eyes and a quiver full of bolts thrown across her back and was admiring one of my swords. The blade, made of obsidian, is one of the sharpest blades in the whole arsenal. The iron pommel has an amethyst stone right below the hilt, set into the eyes of the wolf engraved on it. The twin blades at her side belonged to Damian, a beautiful steel with a gold pommel, another of the wolf blades the eyes set with rubies. Each weapon she chose belonged to one of us.

I walked up to her, taking my blade from her hands and sheathing it to her side. "If you plan on using our weapons, then we're going with you. We have a few calls to make, then we are heading to Mirith." I kissed her cheek, and we walked out of the armory, phones in hand to call our commanders and get the legions ready.

LUNA

My head was spinning. Fennik walked over to the window and looked out at his home. I stood next to him and looked out at the peaceful city. He took a deep breath and turned to me.

"When did you know?" He asked.

"With your brothers? Or about my mom?" I genuinely wasn't sure which question he wanted answered.

"With my brothers. I'm not mad or anything. I just am curious. You make them happy and edgy all at once. I'm sure they told you but we never expected to have a mate. Those three specifically never made it known that they wanted a mate." He looked back out the window.

"Honestly, I don't know. It just kind of happened." I was being honest with him. I wasn't sure when it clicked in place or even if it fully clicked into place yet. I just know that my heart vibrates when they enter a room or when I see them.

"I want to ask them about it, but as the baby, everyone ignores me. When I first saw you, you intrigued me. I'm not sure why, but I wanted to get to know you. When you were attacked by the borg I was worried about you, but what I saw when I looked at Damian screaming for us." He paused and turned to look back at the door. "I could tell what I felt for you was nothing compared to what he felt. The panic I saw, the fear. I wasn't there for your meeting with Bastian, but I saw it when I entered the room. I saw Valyn meeting you and the intrigue in his eyes. I get it. I just envy them for finding their mate and that their mate is you." He smiled at me. I could hear their voices from the hallway.

"You will find your mate, Fennik. I promise when all of this is over that I will help you find your mate. But, I have you to thank for finding me in the first place. They should be thanking you, too." I gave him a big hug, and to my surprise, he hugged me back.

"Now they can't give me hell about my curiosity! Let's go make sure your mom is safe." Fennik laughed and headed for the door. I looked over the room once more. I could do this. I could fight to find my mom, and I could fight for my mates.

CHAPTER 41
LUNA

I wasn't expecting the guys to take me outside to the garden in the courtyard. The fountain was absolutely lovely at night, its stone dancers in the center illuminating under the moonlight. The stars above shone brightly in the sky. I glanced at the princes surrounding me. Each armed to the teeth with knives and swords. Bastian and Damian had their hair pulled back low, Valyn had his up in a man bun. Fennik managed to help me braid my hair back so it wouldn't get in my face if I had to fight.

"Luna, are you ready?" Valyn asked with his hand outstretched toward me. I wounded him by stepping away from his touch earlier. I felt bad. I was aggressive with them all and I didn't mean it. They didn't know my mom was in Mirith. I looked at him and grabbed his hand and nodded.

"Let's go." I smiled at him and looked around at everyone. "So, when do we leave?" Bastian chuckled.

"See that door over there at the back of the house?" He pointed to an oak door with iron hinges and a red blood lily in front of a sun etched into the door. The insignia for Hildaria, I realized. I glanced at Bastian, a little puzzled. "Remember how we got to the summer realm?" he asked me, and I nodded. "Same concept, except this takes us directly into Mirith in Lord Drake's courtyard. It makes meetings easier."

We walked over to the door, and Damian looked at me once more. "Please stay close to us. I know you can protect yourself but, I don't want anything happening to you."

I nodded my head and squeezed Valyn's hand. Fennik stood next to Bastian as Damian opened the door. I could see the blood lilies lining both sides of the sandstone pathway. The fountain in the middle was almost identical to the one we had at Mistveil. Fennik walked through the door first, followed by Damian and Bastian, then Valyn and me. It was warmer here, not by much, but warmer. Footsteps sounded off the stone path in front of us, and the males all gathered around me. Stupid fae dominance.

"Good to see you all." I recognized that voice. I let go of Valyn's hand and pushed Damian and Bastian out of my way, and paused. I saw Nox standing before us, but he wasn't alone. Behind him stood a tall, blonde, muscular man. I would know that man anywhere. The man I had once told myself I would marry. Virgil was in Mirith standing behind Nox, looking directly into me, or at the necklace around my neck.

"Virgil?" I asked, looking at him now didn't make my heart stutter and there was no butterfly feeling in my stomach. I didn't feel like a child about to be scolded or an idiot girl following around her stupid crush. It was nice. He blinked a few times and shook his head, moving his attention from my neck to my eyes. I don't think he even realized that I had spoken to him.

"Luna? Is that really you? What are you doing here?" Panic laced his words, and he rushed to grab me. I stepped back behind Bastian, who immediately put his arm out, keeping me behind him. Twin, low warning growls came from behind me. I realized Damian and Valyn had taken up positions behind me.

"If I were you, I wouldn't try to touch her again." Valyn glanced at Nox. "Prince Nox, is your father home?" Valyn stepped in front of us, eyes shooting daggers at Virgil. Why in the hell was Virgil even here?

"Luna, what is going on? Come over here. We have to talk, please." Virgil was ignoring the clear warning that Valyn had just given him as he reached out to me again. He took another step forward, but it was Nox who halted his advances this time.

"What are you doing here?" I asked, moving to the side of Bastian but still not taking Virgil's hand. Damian's hand rested on my lower back, sending a warm, soothing heat through my body.

"Are you kidding me Luna? It's only been a few weeks. Have you even been home? You don't want to talk to me in private, fine." He pulled down the collar of his black shirt. A scar, still fresh, I realized, was in the middle of his chest, far too close to his heart. "Your idiot brother had a knife to Nox's throat and my dumbass snuck up behind him and grabbed him. I spun him around, not thinking, and next thing I know I'm in pain and bleeding. I didn't think he would've put a knife in me. Guess I was wrong." He let go of the collar of his shirt and it snapped back into place.

"Luther did that to you?! Why did he have a knife to your throat Nox?!" I was screaming. Everyone called him prince. Why? I felt another hand rest on my lower back. I caught the sight of black hair out of my peripheral. Bastian was trying to help Damian ground me.

"Virgil saved my life, so I brought him here and saved his. This way, there is no life debt. He is supposed to still be in bed, resting. However, the attack started, and he refused to stay in bed. As for Luther, he was telling me to keep away from you." Nox stepped forward and looked at me. "You and I have to talk."

Damian and Bastian flanked both of my sides, and Valyn stepped back in front of me. Stupid territorial Fae idiots. I pushed them out of the way and moved in front of Valyn. "He's not going to hurt me, so stop acting like that." I said to my princes as I walked over towards

Nox. Footsteps sounded down the path behind Nox and Virgil, and they both turned around and bowed.

The princes behind me bowed. I, however, did not. I have never bowed to Lord Drake. He had never asked me to or made me. "Please, enough with the bowing. I assume you all are up to speed about what's going on." Lord Drake smiled at me as he walked up. "Hello Luna, please don't tell me they're allowing you to fight?"

"We have very little choice, your highness. She didn't give us many options. It was either we bring her, or she was going to attempt to cross the Mitos herself." Damian spoke from behind me. I turned around and shot him a look that if I had the power would've knocked him on his ass.

"She literally wanted to come here the moment she heard the attack on Mirith. She's here to protect what you told her was here." Bastian walked around me and leaned up against the stone wall. I didn't like the tone he was using.

"Ah, your mother. She is safe, Luna. I would never, ever let anything happen to her. You're more than welcome to go see her." Lord Drake reached his hand out for me to take. Why in the hell did everyone want to hold my hand today? Everyone was staring at me, and I didn't like it. I closed my eyes and took a deep breath.

"I need a few moments alone." I said, and I turned and walked away from the group. I walked over to where the blood lilies were the brightest. I took in their floral smell, inhaling slowly, exhaling even slower. My mind was racing, and I needed to calm down. So much was going on all at once that I was reeling. I wanted to go see my mother, but I want to protect those who can't. I at least can fight, and I can be helpful. The smell of a campfire swirled around me. I didn't need to turn around to know who was behind me. "I said I needed a few moments alone, Fennik."

"I know, but out of everyone over there, I'm probably the only one less on edge. I think they might kill your friend if he tries to touch you again." He came up beside me and looked out over the blood lilies. "Before this week, I hadn't been here in a long time. I forgot how beautiful it is here."

"When we came up to the castle back home, I saw blood lilies mixed with sapphire blooms. I thought they were native to the Hildaria region. Why are they in Mistveil?" I glanced at Fennik. He was right, he was less on edge than any of them by the fountain.

"It was an offering during the first big war between fae and the demons in the south. Hildaria gave us the blood lilies to plant with our sapphire blooms as a show of allegiance and friendship." He looked over the sprawling garden once more. "I always found them beautiful. Lord Drake has always been kind to us, and Prince Nox has always been like a brother of sorts. A bit of a pain in the ass, but he's nice."

"How long has it been since you've been here?" I wonder if he was here when I was little. There used to be a guy who came around when I would visit who kind of looked like Fennik, but he wasn't as nice.

"It's been about 20 years since I was last here. I was visiting Prince Nox about an ongoing battle he was in. I didn't know your father and Prince Nox were so close. I'm sorry." Fennik looked back at everyone. They gathered around the fountain talking about something, most likely pertaining to the attack this morning.

"I think I might have seen someone who looked like you here before. I was here roughly about 12 years ago. I visited every summer with my siblings. Until I was three, I thought Mirith was my home. I thought I belonged here until my father came and gathered us up. My mother went back and forth between us and here. I only came back during the summer and only for about a month. My mother brought all of us here. Lilly and I loved this place. Luther didn't care for the place much. He said it was too quiet and too calm for his liking. It's not the bustling of Celvenia." I sighed. Did Luther honestly stab Virgil?

Soft footsteps came up behind us and Fennik turned around and let out a low whistle. "I think I need to let this person speak to you, for I fear my fur being singled off. Just be true to you, okay? That's all that matters and if you need a few moments to gather yourself after whatever this is, I got you." Fennik patted me on the shoulder and walked away.

"I'm sorry if I upset you at all. I just really needed to talk to you about what happened." Nox didn't walk up to me. He kept back a few feet, as if he was afraid to get closer to me.

"What is it, Nox? Clearly, there is something we need to talk about. Like how my father supposedly raised you from a hatchling?" I spoke calmly, evenly.

"Yeah, about that. I've been with him since he got with your mother. He didn't raise me, more like I kept him alive because your mom asked me to. Mind if I sit next to you?" He asked me as if I was gonna rip his head off. I patted the wall next to me. He walked over and leaned against the waist-high wall that split the courtyard from the garden. "Look, I'm sorry, okay? I told you the truth when I said your house was full of death. I also kept my promise to keep Virgil safe. Although, I think your feelings about him might have changed significantly." He looked over at the princes and Virgil. They all looked at ease, more so than when I was standing there.

"They might've. Thank you for saving him, though. I still wouldn't want him dead." I glanced at Nox and forced a smile. "What else?"

"Have you ever thought about why you differ from the rest of your family? The hair, the eyes, any of it?" He looked over at the gathered group. I nodded my head. It wasn't anything I hadn't thought of before. Why in the world would he ask me that, though? Why did it matter to him about me?

"Of course, I think about it. It doesn't matter though; my family is my family." He looked at me once more. As much as I wanted to beat the hell out of Luther right now. Lilly was safe, alive, and well with Kira and Harper.

"Do you ever wonder why your mother came here of all places to get help and not Mistveil? Why risk coming all the way here?" Nox rattled off question after question as if I should've known the answers. I wondered the same things, but I thought nothing about them because I was always being told I didn't know what I was talking about.

Before I could respond, a loud roaring came from the sky above the courtyard, the sky going dark above us. Nox pushed me between his back and the stone wall. The roaring became louder as a large dual headed black and white dragon came into view. I shoved Nox away and went for the crossbow on my back and loaded a bolt into it. I lined up the sight and steadied my breath. Niklaus came running out from the castle yelling something I ignored. I took a deep breath; the sun glinted off the shining silver armor of the rider atop the dragon. A blue cape billowed behind the rider, the dragon reared back and dove straight for us. I saw the dual horned helm of the rider and shot.

The bolt hit the helm, knocking the riders' head back, leaving the helm to fall from their head. The blonde hair beneath the helm nearly stopped my heart. The beard was exactly how it was the last I saw him. Luther was the rider on top of the humongous dual headed dragon. Luther was leading the attack on Mirith. What in the hell was he doing? Virgil was on my right before I could blink.

"Is that Luther?!" Shock overcame him as quickly as it took hold of me. Disbelief plagued me, but I couldn't let him get close. I pulled another bolt out of the quiver and latched it into the crossbow, taking aim. Virgil grabbed at the crossbow, pulling it down towards the ground. "Are you kidding me Luna? That's your brother!" He yelled at me. I pushed him back and aimed the bow at him.

"Never touch me again." I snarled, taking aim back at Luther. I shot the second bolt at his chest. It ricocheted off of him and landed on the dragon's back.

"Luna, why are you doing this?" Virgil was on his knees, gazing up at me as if finally seeing the real me. Not the simpering girl who would follow him everywhere, done anything for him. No, I would never be that woman again.

"He stabbed you Virgil! He held a knife to Nox's throat! You're okay with letting him get away with that? I'm tired of being used and kept weak. I am not weak and it's about time you all realized that." I shouted at him. Infuriated as I was, I wouldn't let him win. Nox was at my side a moment later. I heard yelling in the distance and knew my princes were heading my way.

"Want a lift?" Nox asked, winking at me. I knew exactly what he meant.

"I'm not a dragon rider, Nox. I will only slow you down." I shook my head and glanced at my princes who were running towards me. The look of admiration on their faces was enough to melt my heart. Lord Drake was saying something to Fennik and Niklaus. Damian's head was on a swivel between me and Lord Drake. Growls came from outside the courtyard walls and Bastian and Damian smiled viciously. Their beasts have arrived. They awaited acknowledgment from me, and I nodded. They were off in a blink of an eye. Valyn blew me a kiss and headed for the sea. His host must be close by as well.

"Let's get airborne," Nox smiled at me and looked up at Luther before adding, "little sis."

CHAPTER 42
LUNA

"Excuse me?" I must've heard him wrong. Maybe he means it in the friend way. Like sees me as a little sister. Yeah, that makes better sense to me.

"You heard me little sis. Let's go." In a blink of an eye, Nox grabbed me and flung me onto his back. He started running and before I knew it, the muscular man beneath me was shifting. Black shiny scales began erupting from the dragon tattoo on his arm, covering his whole body. Large wings sprouted out of his back from his shoulder blades. That had to be extremely painful. His face elongated and the horns on his head came into view. Nox was a gigantic dragon. His wingspan was almost as wide as the courtyard itself, which was huge. Nox huffed. I gripped onto what I thought was his shoulder.

"This is insane!" I shouted over the wind whipping at my braid. The blades at my sides clanked off each other. I wonder if he could talk like this.

"Yes, I can talk. So, you may want to watch what you're thinking." Nox swiped in low and grabbed something off the ground and tossed it up into the air. "Be careful. I'm gonna have that land right below where you're lying." I gripped tighter into him, and he slowed his pace as I realized he grabbed a rider's saddle.

"How in the hell am I supposed to secure that?" It landed with a thud. I saw no straps, but it settled into place on its own. Magic, I realized. Dragons had magic, too. Not as strong as a Fae, but strong enough. "Ok, I get it. You're strong."

"Get into the saddle and get ready. They're going to head right for us. We're gonna take them for a ride." I lowered down Nox's back and got into the saddle. This was not like riding a horse. I was shaking more than I did my first time riding a horse. Dragon riders usually stood on the saddles, but I had nothing to grip onto and my luck I would fall right off.

"Just stand and stop having an internal debate, please." He spoke calmly, wait a minute. I heard him in my mind? Seriously? "Yes, seriously. Dragons have connections with their riders, a mental bond, if you will. It's part of our powers. Stand on the saddle. You don't need to hold on to any reins or anything like that. I won't lose you."

So basically, I just have to think, and it's like talking to you directly? I thought to myself, thinking how ridiculous this sounded.

"Yes, that's exactly how it works." Nox kept his slow pace until I let bravery and adrenaline kick in and stood. The saddle constricted around my feet and held me in place.

That is incredible. No wonder my father loved riding. This is a rush on its own. Nox, I have a question. Why did you call me little sis?

"Because that's what you are to me. Not because of Gunther either, so get that thought out of your head before it even enters." He picked up speed as he spoke down through the mental bond.

What do you mean? Wouldn't he be the only reason you would see me as family? There isn't any other connection. Is there? He picked up the pace and turned straight upward. A rolling wave of nausea threatened to escape from me. We were heading right for Luther and the massive dragon he rode. I gripped onto my crossbow tighter and locked a bolt into place. My eyes watered a bit but I could still focus.

"Put that down. We're not going to fight them here. They're gonna chase us to the Kilspur ocean where Valyns naval unit will aid us." We got closer to them, and Nox huffed once more. He put his feet out and kicked at Luther's dragon, using the force to propel us out towards the Kilspur. I looked back and sure enough, they were following us.

I think we need to push it. It looks like you pissed them off. Of course, you could always let me shoot at them. I'm a fantastic shot. I beamed at him. Speaking mentally was most definitely creepy. I aimed my crossbow again at Luther. I needed to drop Luther off that damn dragon.

Nox dropped suddenly, and a bolt whizzed right where my head was moments ago. Luther was shooting at me? I glanced up at where Luther and his dragon were. He was loading up another bolt.

Still want me to put it away? I barked at Nox. I aimed my crossbow and fired, direct hit, just not at Luther. The bolt went straight through the two-toned dragon's right wing, making it lose its balance. I quickly reached for another bolt. I have five left. I need to make them count. I locked the next bolt in place and aimed at the other wing. I pulled the trigger and again it struck true. The dragon lost its balance and fell towards the ground. I could hear Luther yelling something from the saddle. I didn't know if it was at me or the dragon below him.

Nox sprang down after Luther and the dragon, mistake number one. The black and white dragon leveled out and regained its speed, heading straight for us. Nox tried to dodge away from the other dragon as it swiped out at him. I felt my feet loosen from the saddle. I hooked another bolt into the crossbow and aimed again as Nox regain his balance. The dragon flipped back around and was coming straight for us. I took the shot. The bolt sailed right past the dragon's right side of the white head. Three more bolts left. I had another bolt in place and aimed again, striking the left eye of the black head. It roared and Nox raced straight for the belly of the dragon, biting at what I would assume was its lower abdomen.

We need to get further out to the sea. I thought to myself, the smell of iron was thick in the surrounding air.

"That last attack should do the trick." Nox spoke into my mind. "Hold on tight." I could hear the smile in his words. He flapped his mighty wings once, twice. By the third time, we were a good distance away from the dual headed dragon. I could see the glimmering deep blue water of the Kilspur in the distance coming closer with every flap of Nox's wings. The view up here was beautiful. The trees were a dazzling array of golds, reds, and oranges. Autumn was practically in full bloom here. However, the one thing I wish I had thought of was how cold it would be this close to the sea. I saw what I could only assume was Valyns naval unit in the distance. The town below us was still smoldering, some buildings left in rubble. The rebuilding would take some time. I heard a whistling sound before I felt anything.

A sharp pain shot through my left leg. I screamed out in pain as a bolt shot through me. "What the hell?" Nox yelled down the bond. Blood streamed down my leg. I had to pull the bolt out quickly and stop the bleeding. I hooked the crossbow to my back and ripped off a piece of fabric from the sleeve of my shirt. I tied it around my leg right above the wound as tight as I could. Grabbing the bolt, I let out another scream. Ripping the bolt from my leg, I tossed it off the side of Nox. Shit! I hope that doesn't hit anyone!

That asshole just shot me! I thought back to Nox. I ripped another piece of my sleeve off and wrapped it tightly around the holes. This is gonna hurt like hell.

"He is going to die!" Nox snarled. I pray to Vanalli that we make it to the sea before I get shot again. I retrieved my crossbow from my back and locked another bolt into place. There was a soft spot in Luther's armor right where the shoulder plates met with the breast plate. If I can hit him there, he won't be able to fire another shot. Steadying my breathing, I took aim once more. Nox must've heard my thoughts because he steadied his own breathing. There was the sweet spot. I released the trigger and prayed the bolt struck true.

I heard a yell from above the other dragon. Luther was screaming in agony. Good, let him try to fix that on the back of an angry, pissed off dragon. *Nox, we need to hurry!* He picked up his speed again; the beach coming into view. I could hear guttural growling from beneath us, my heart sunk. There were two smaller dragons flying in below us. With only one bolt left, I wouldn't be able to do much from his back. I attached the final bolt into the crossbow and aimed towards the smallest of the dragons. *Please don't let this be a child.*

"He's not a child. He's just short. Take the shot!" Nox's words of reassurance definitely helped me. I aimed right where the head met the neck and shot. The small blue dragon went down, the rider on top falling off and down beneath the beast.

The other dragon, a dark purple one, was coming closer to us. I spent all of my bolts; I attached Valyn's crossbow to the saddle horn and thought to Nox. *I'm going to drop onto the other one and take it out hand to hand.*

"The hell you are!" He snarled at me. I guess he didn't realize that my feet were already loose from the saddle. I stepped a foot off the saddle, then the next. I started running down the length of his spine. Luther and his dragon were still flying behind us, but they slowed significantly. I can do this. I sprinted at full speed and jumped off Nox's tail. I seriously didn't think this through. Free falling from one dragon to the next was probably not the smartest idea.

I pulled Damians twin blades from my side as I fell, focusing on the dragon below me. Out of the corner of my eyes, I saw something coming right for me. Flying as quick as its little wings would take it, a golden-brown eagle looked as if it was racing me towards the dragon. I ignored it and aimed my blades for the rider. A flash of light burst into the sky and a muscular blonde male appeared before me. Niklaus was now diving headfirst, blade at the ready towards the dragon itself. He landed before me, driving his silver blade down into the right wing of the dragon before shifting back into the eagle and flying high again. My blades met the helm of the dragon rider, making the loudest clanging sound. His head knocked back, the helm falling off. He looked as if he couldn't be no older than Luther. Raven black hair and ice blue eyes looked at me in disbelief. He drew his sword as Niklaus landed another blow to the left wing of the dragon. The rider left the safety of his saddle and charged at me. I dodged out of the first strike, deflecting the blade back at him. I lunged one blade down but then side stepped and shoved the other blade into the thigh of the man. He went down but didn't scream, no he smiled at me. What the hell? I looked down at my blade and saw an oily blue slime where blood should be.

"Someone like you will not easily take me down." He spoke as if the wind was carrying his words to me.

"What the hell are you?" I aimed my blades back at him. Maybe if I aimed for an artery, he would drop.

"I am what most people would consider a nightmare. Not a daemon, not a fae. We are from the Royalty of Hell itself. You may call me a Hilmer. A nameless creature who is here to take back what once was ours." He charged at me again. I tried to run but my leg gave out. I crossed the twin blades above me just in time to catch his blade.

"If you're a Hilmer, are you the ones behind this false war?" I said through gritted teeth. He laughed, a grating sound to my ears. I looked up at him through the blades. The once blue eyes were now fully black, soulless. It hit me right in that moment. "You're using this man's body!" I shouted at him.

"You are very observant. It's a shame that the others in this world aren't as observant as you, Princess." He pushed the blade down further into mine. I didn't notice his other hand move and retrieve a knife from his side. He slashed the knife down the front of my arm. "You smell delicious. What are you?" Something flicked into his eyes.

"I am human." I snapped at him as I withdrew the one blade and lunged it straight into his side. More blue oily slime coated my hands, making my grip slowly slip. I pulled it out and pushed back as he doubled over.

Niklaus dropped onto the dragon behind the Hilmer, blade angled at the head of the dragon. "What in the hell is going on?" He slowly pushed the blade into the dragon's neck right where the head and neck met. We started dropping out of the sky.

"He's a Hilmer!" I screamed over the wind at Niklaus. His eyes widened. He quickly withdrew his sword and angled it back towards the Hilmer. I got back onto my feet, putting Damian's twin blades back on my side. I grabbed Bastian's blade from my other side and angled it at the front of the Hilmer. Howling came from below us; we could hear screams, howls and growls. The clashing of swords and steel sang up to us as we were falling through the clouds. The Hilmer laughed again.

"You two will not kill me. You can't." He looked at me and smiled. "The Ritmers will be very interested in you." Before I could ask why or even retort to the Hilmer, Niklaus beheaded him. I shoved the blade into the heart of the Hilmer, saying a prayer to Vanalli to save the soul of the man whose body was possessed.

"How are we going to get down from here without dying?" I don't know how the hell we were still standing, but the ground was coming faster that I liked.

"Trust me?" Niklaus asked as he walked close to me. Something told me not to trust him, but I had no choice. I nodded my head. "Good, now close your eyes." As I shut my eyes, I felt his hand on my back guiding me. Before I knew it, the dragon beneath my feet was gone and I was falling faster. *Did he just shove me off the dragon?!* Panic set in, but I couldn't open my eyes. I heard a loud growl in my ear and felt large claws grab me. The smell of rotting flesh and iron filled my nose. *This is it, I'm gonna die.*

"Open your eyes, Luna." I recognized that voice. I felt the rough hands grip my waist and remove me from the claws that were holding me gently, I now realized. I opened my eyes and saw Damian, covered in blood and hair, a matted mess. I grabbed his face and kissed him. I didn't care that he was covered in blood. I had blood all over myself, as well.

"Where is Bastian? Valyn?" I looked around and finally took in the sight of the scaled beasts around me. Large fangs and claws were everywhere. Blood, both red and blue, flooded the streets. No wonder Damian was covered from head to toe. In the middle of the claws, fur, scales and fangs was Bastian swinging his broad sword around, striking all those in his reach. He looked over at me and smiled as he drove the sword into the chest of a man. More oily blue slime flowed out of the body as it dropped to the ground.

"Why were you free falling off a dragon?" Damian got my attention again, checking me over, noticing my leg and my arm. I had almost forgotten to be pissed.

"Your asshole brother shoved me off." I pointed over at the golden-brown eagle that was flashing between bird and fae.

A siren sounded from the sea. Bastian ran towards us, "Come on, we have to move. Now!" He grabbed me and threw me on his back as he shifted into his wolf, and we took off deeper into the city. Damian and Niklaus were close behind.

"Where is Fennik?" I asked him as we raced through the streets. I looked up and saw Nox was following us inland, but Luther and his dragon were nowhere to be found. Good, let him bleed out somewhere.

"He's back at the castle. He is better with healing magic than the rest of us, aside from Niklaus." Bastian said, still unnerving to have animals talk to me, but whatever I'll get used to it.

Another siren sounded. The ground beneath us shook. Miriths castle came into view just up ahead. Civilians who had no magic were being rushed into the castle gates, while those with magic stood outside the gates holding off the Hilmer army. The siren sounded again as everyone made it inside the gate. We reached it just in time to follow the magic wielders into the gates before they closed up behind us. A whistle sounded from the sea, followed by the ground vigorously shaking. To my horror they started bombing the city.

CHAPTER 43
LUNA

Smoke filled the sky, the screams of beasts, and dragons filled the air. Lord Drake and others started ushering civilians into the castle. Nox landed on the castle wall, shifting and yelling orders at the soldiers on the parapet. The sky turned red and black; the fires blazing bright. I scanned the courtyard, looking for everyone. Fennik was helping heal an elderly woman who was bleeding from the head. Bastian was up on the wall with Damian and Nox ordering soldiers of fae and beasts alike. Virgil was helping take the injured to Fennik. Niklaus was staring at me from across the courtyard. I headed straight for him. My arm and leg were stinging with every step I took.

"Why in the hell did you shove me off the dragon?" I yelled at him as I got closer. He looked past me towards the stairs that led up to the castle wall.

"You really want to know?" Niklaus looked at my arm and leg. "You're bleeding, sit." He grabbed my good arm and forced me to sit on a small stone wall around a small garden. He grabbed my arm and put two fingers at the top of the cut. His hand glowed a bright green, illuminating the wound beneath. He trailed his fingers down the length of the cut from my elbow to right above my wrist. "You're lucky," he said. "If this was on the other side of your arm, you'd be dead." He let go of my arm and looked down at my leg, tugging gently at the strips of fabric. He looked at me with a question in his eyes.

"My idiot brother shot me." I looked at my arm and then back at Niklaus. He covered the wound with both of his hands and the green light shined again. This time, a warmth came with the light. He pulled his hands away and sat back on the ground, a bead of sweat dripping down from his forehead. "Thank you." I muttered.

"Your body already started the healing process. I was just able to speed things up a bit." He wiped the sweat away and stood up. "If you want to see why I pushed you, follow me." He headed for the stairway behind him that lead up the wall. I got up, testing out the strength of my leg. It didn't hurt. Honestly, it felt great. I followed Niklaus up the narrow staircase to a wooden door at the top. He opened it, and the smoke and ash burned my eyes. We walked out of the stairwell and onto the main walkway, heading towards the others.

"Niklaus. What did you mean when you said my body had already started the healing process?" I asked him curiously. Humans had a very slow recovery rate with bones and things of that nature.

"You truly don't know, do you?" He stopped and turned around. I shrugged my shoulders. "I could scent it from the moment I met you. There is a reason you didn't need long to recover from the Borg attack. The others have an idea, but they don't have a way to explain it. Truthfully neither do I but, Luna, you are fae."

"I can't be fae, Niklaus. My parents are human. Unless a human giving birth on fae land gives me fae abilities, I'm not." Why in the world were people here convinced I was a fae? "What scent are you talking about? Do I smell bad or something?"

He laughed, "Not at all. It's actually enticing. You have this ethereal wind smell to you. Like the wind after a storm or the forest after a long rainfall. Either way, you may not want to believe it, but you are fae Luna." He turned and walked towards the high rise of the wall. "That is why I shoved you off." He pointed in towards what looked to be a temple. A long spire, on top of a marble white building, with pillars and gold banners hanging at the entrance. The long, once white stone steps leading up to the doors were now colored red by blood. A top of the spire laid the impaled body of the dragon we had just been fighting on.

"You knew it was going to land there?" The disbelief in my voice must've been all over my face.

"You don't have wings. I do. Luckily, one of Damian's beasts realized you weren't an enemy and saved you." He shrugged and turned from me.

"You mean you didn't have a plan if they decided I was an enemy?" I was so pissed; I grabbed a stone from the ground and chucked it at his head. It hit him and dropped to the ground. Bastian's head turned in our direction. "I could've died!" I shouted.

"Yeah, well, you didn't so see. All's well that ends well." Niklaus's hand rubbed his head where the stone hit. He picked up the stone and tossed it over the side of the wall. "Is that how you repay someone for helping you? Throwing stones at them?" He laughed and continued walking towards his brothers.

"You're lucky I don't shove you off the wall." I pushed past him and walked straight for Bastian and Damian. I didn't even notice Virgil had come up onto the wall and was standing next to Nox. As I got closer, I saw the carnage outside the wall. Bodies were everywhere, beasts, dragons, humans and fae alike. The fires were being held at bay by the magic wielders who harnessed the power of the waters, courtesy of the gift from Undine herself. I looked back at the males in front of me. "Who was gonna tell me I smell like wind and rain? Oh, and that you all think I am fae." I glowered at them.

"I thought me calling you little sis was enough for you to figure it out." Nox looked at me, that sarcastic ass smile plastered on his face.

"You're a dragon! Not fae!" I screamed. My body was burning from the inside out. Anger raised through me. They all just looked at me wide eyed. A bright gold light was surrounding the area where we stood.

"Luna, I need you to calm down. You're burning a little too bright." Lord Drake walked up the stairs behind me. I was so confused, burning too bright? My head started pounding and my sight blurred. "Luna, breathe."

My body started shaking. The roaring in my head was so loud. I felt hands on my shoulders, but I couldn't tell who was touching me. A sharp pain went through my head from ear to ear and everything went black. I couldn't hear anything or see anything. The darkness surrounded me and I felt like I was drifting in water. The pain became a dull throbbing in the distance. It was like I was separate from my body.

A bright golden flame came into my vision. As it got closer to me, I could make out the details. It was a male figure now standing in front of me. I couldn't make out the eyes or the hair, but the smile looked so familiar.

Hello Luna. You have been burning so brightly lately. Have you figured out the truth yet? The figure's voice was like a harp, elegant and beautiful.

What truth? That I am Fae? I asked the figure, surprised to hear my own voice sound so elegant.

Yes, he smiled at me, *but have you found out why?*

Why am I fae? I don't know, but everyone keeps telling me I am. I don't get it. I don't look fae in the slightest. Frustration was seeping out of me. *I wish everyone would just be honest with me.*

Everyone is being honest with you. You just don't want to hear it. Your father is someone you know. Gunther is not your father. But, Lilliana, your mother is my daughter. She is both fae and a goddess, I granted her the ability to disguise her identity so that she could see where her love would go with Gunther. Clearly, that turned into one child. But you, you are the product of her and her true mate. The mate she stayed with when Gunther sent her away after discovering her true identity. The figure stepped closer to me.

Wait, my father didn't send my mother away. She had three children with him. She only left us to get help for Lilly! I was getting angry. This thing knew nothing of me and my family.

He smiled at me. *No, Gunther again is not your father. You are from the blood of fae royalty and a goddess. Gunther betrayed your mother after you were born by having an affair with her best friend. She planned to leave him with you and come back to Mirith to live, but her friend became pregnant. She stayed for her friend. When Lilly was born, Lilliana's friend died from complications of childbirth. Your mother stayed to raise the love child of her husband and her best friend. Your mother revealed her identity to Gunther after Lilly turned 5 and showed the first sign of the graying. Gunther threatened Lilliana that if she didn't leave and never return, he would tell his commanding officer what she really was. She would've been exiled from both Celvenia and the fae lands for deceiving him.* He shook his head. *My daughter loved him, and he returned her love with hate and heartbreak. He deserves the curse of the graying. Lilly, however, does not. She made it back to Mirith and has been here waiting and hoping to see you again. But be warned, those who have the graying or are the offspring of someone who has the graying are vessels.*

I don't understand. Vessels for what? Am I disguised then too?

They are Vessels for deamons and Hilmers, they will be easily possessed. And yes, you are, but since you have been on fae land for more than a few days, your true powers and form are trying to break free. My darling granddaughter, you are currently burning bright like a star, changing into your true self. It's going to be a big adjustment, but when you wake up, you will be where you were. Surrounded by family and your mates. Love them and let them guide you. Hug your mother for me.

I will see you all soon.

Wait! Who are you? I reached for him.

He chuckled; *I am Undas. I'll let your mother tell you who your grandmother is. It's time to wake up Luna.*

CHAPTER 44
LUNA

I tried to blink my eyes open. The smell of smoke and ash was still choking my senses. Shadows moved around me. Slowly, my eyes adjusted to the light. The burning I felt before being taken by darkness subsided, but everything was now brighter and louder.

"Luna! Luna!" Bastian was yelling my name, extremely loud.

"Will you stop yelling her name? She isn't deaf, she just passed out." Nox's annoying voice chimed in.

"Both of you knock it off. Look at her. She went through the changing." Damian's voice was crystal clear. The serious tone was alarming.

"She's his daughter. If I were you, I would let him see her." Niklaus said from a distance. I heard footsteps shuffle away from me and a set of steps come forward.

"Open your eyes, Luna." I knew that voice all too well. The man who always treated me like I was special, the man who always treated me like his own. Wait a minute, Niklaus just said I'm his daughter. Does that mean that Lord Drake is my father?!

"Undas." I said, opening my eyes and looking at Lord Drake. His eyes widened, but he calmed down his reaction and smiled at me.

"So, you really saw him then? Your powers manifested like his. I bet he was so proud of that." He chuckled. "Well then, I assume he filled you in about me and your mother then?"

"He didn't tell me you were my father. He just said I was born of fae royalty and a goddess. You just filled in the blank. Or should I say Niklaus did?" I sat up and smiled, looking at two of my mates. "I'm just glad the fae royalty was you." He laughed and helped me up. A thought screamed in my head, "Wait! Undas said that those who have the graying or are offspring of someone who has caught the graying are vessels for deamons and Hilmers. They can be possessed easily."

A deep male laugh came from the wall just ahead of us. A chill scurried down my spine. Clanking of armored boots clinked off of the stone, a long royal blue cape flowed in the wind. The only thing different from the last time I saw General Rothsberg was the blood leaking out of his armor. He slowly started clapping, "Luna, nice to see you finally showing your true colors. Gunther talked about how Lilliana left him for a fae after Luther was born and came back with you." He looked behind him. "See, I told you I wasn't lying to you. You sister," he spat at me, "Isn't really your sister. Lilly is your only true sister."

"Don't lie. Our mother is the same. The only blood you share with Lilly is Gunther's. Just as the only blood you share with me is our mothers. Which means you and I are half siblings, whereas the only sibling I was truly close with isn't even my blood, but she treated me better than you. I now understand why he treated me so bad. I can understand it. I don't like it, but I understand it. So, what's your excuse?" I looked past Vikrum and directly at Luther.

"You shot at me Luna. Why?" Luther looked at me with hurt in his eyes.

"Dude really? You're asking me why I shot at you. Let's see, last time we saw each other, you acted like a massive dick. You stabbed Virgil after threatening Prince Nox, yes Luther, Prince Nox. Oh, and you literally attacked me and Nox. I shot a warning shot when you had your helm on. I didn't know it was you. When I noticed it was you, I was more pissed off." I stormed up to the General. "King Harold did not bring this war on. You did. You're the one pulling the strings." I shoved the General into Luther.

Bastian and Damian were at my side within seconds. Virgil and Nox took up the flank. My father was behind us. I drew Bastian's swords from my side. Each of the princes did the same thing. Virgil had his knives out palmed in each hand. I didn't know when Valyn and Fennik had made it to the wall, coming up behind Vikrum and Luther.

"See, Luther, you belong with us. They're quick to kill you, not to talk this out." Vikrum spoke back to Luther. He grabbed Luther's hand and shoved something in it. "We will take great care of him." He laughed.

Luther looked at me, his blue eyes fading to black. He smirked and took a deep breath in. "Next time I won't aim for your leg." He walked up to the ledge. "Get ready, sis. This is only the beginning." Vikrum smiled and jumped off the ledge. I couldn't help the scream that escaped from me as Luther winked at me and followed Vikrum off the ledge. I tried to run for the ledge, but Lord Drake grabbed my wrist.

"Don't!" He yelled as he pulled me back towards him.

Without warning, the dual headed white and black dragon flew up the side of the wall with Luther in the saddle, taking off towards the Kilspur.

Nox looked at Lord Drake. "Do we follow?"

"No. We need to gain control of the situation here and assess the risks and the damages. They're both injured. They won't be able to get help from a healer. Get any one wounded to Listhrum and The Mor. Let's get you inside. We will discuss more once the citizens have been taken care of. Boys, if you don't mind. Please escort my daughter inside. Miriam will find you a room to freshen up." He handed me off to Valyn. Tears streamed down my face as my father let go of me. My world was spiraling, and I couldn't get it to stop. Luther wasn't himself anymore and I don't know if there was anything left of the brother I knew in there.

"It's okay Luna. We will save him. We all saw it, the change in his eyes. We just have to figure out what Rothsberg shoved into his hand. Either way, we will find a way to bring him back." Valyn pulled me in close to him and let me bury my face in his chest. He lifted me up into his arms and carried me down the stairs and across the courtyard into the castle.

He was right, whatever the General shoved into his hands changed him. Took over him. I will gut that bastard before I let him hurt Luther. Asshole or not. More shouting came from in front of us and behind us. This was only the beginning of the war, a small victory.

CHAPTER 45
LUNA

They filled the castle with the civilians of the city. Screams of the wounded echoed off the walls, children crying for their parents, and men arguing. A young blonde woman in all black walked up to us. "This way." She ushered us down a quieter hallway. Two large double doors with the Hildaria insignia were at the end, with a smaller door off to the left.

"That is the restroom. Feel free to freshen up in there." She opened the double doors to a large meeting room. A long oak table was in the center of the room, shelves of books upon books lined the walls. Maps littered the top of the table with what looked like little chest pieces arranged all over it. Pens and compasses lay scattered everywhere. This place really needed to be tidied up a bit. There were several plush red velvet chairs surrounding the room. By the window sat a red velvet couch. Probably the best spot for reading. I pictured my mom lounged about on the couch reading one of her favorite books. This place seemed so much like something she would've done in our house back in Celvenia.

"His Majesty will be with you shortly." She bowed as she walked out the door, closing it behind her.

Bastian, Damian and Valyn walked with me over to the couch. I dropped my weapons on the floor next to us. Niklaus, Fennik and Virgil took a seat in the chairs by the table. I sat down on the large couch and sighed.

"You said Undas. What did Lord Drake mean by you met him?" Bastian asked, and everyone turned towards me.

"When I blacked out, I saw darkness. I couldn't hear any of you or see any of you. But a golden fiery figure came to me. He told me his name was Undas and said that he was my grandfather. My mother's father, but he wouldn't tell me who my grandmother is. He said he would leave that to my mother to tell me." I shook my head.

"So, we are mated to the granddaughter of the God of Fire. Well, that sure as hell explains the golden fire I saw in the sea when you were attacked by the mermaids." Valyn said nonchalantly.

"Excuse me, what?!" Fennik yelled from the chair. "When the hell were you attacked by mermaids?"

"A few days ago, don't worry, she's fine." Bastian smiled, but I knew that was just because he was still upset about it.

"Shit, so they are real?" Virgil ran his hand through his messy blonde hair.

"Yeah, and they are assholes." I laughed. He chuckled with me, but things were still awkward. We would have to address that, but not now. The doors opened suddenly, and Nox came stalking into the room.

"Everyone who was injured in the attack is currently being seen between Lithstrum and The Mor. Maggie and Bethany will have everyone taken care of and back on their feet soon. The contractors and construction workers have already started looking at blueprints and are looking for materials to rebuild the city. It's going to take some time, but at least people are already eager to rebuild." Nox took a seat around the table.

"Glad to see you started filling in everyone." Lord Drake said as he walked in and looked at me. I rose immediately from my seat. "Sit down Luna. You're still not used to your new body. It will take some time, but we will work on it together. As for everything else, we will fix it all in time. I already sent word to Athena to inform the King of the situation." Lord Drake took a seat at the head of the table and looked over the maps.

I sat back down, letting my head rest on the back of the couch, and closed my eyes. I let the sounds of the workers outside fill my ears. Everyone was shouting about materials and finding their loved ones. I took a deep breath and opened my eyes as Lord Drake cleared his throat.

"If I don't get you to the throne room soon, I have a feeling your mother is going to barge through those doors and start beating people." He rubbed his temples. "I told her she needed to wait just a little longer to see you. Honestly, I'm surprised she didn't threaten me when I told her that." He laughed a little.

"As much as I don't want to wait any longer to see her, what are we going to do about everything?" I asked. Damian rubbed my back. I was sore and felt dirty.

"We are already starting to rebuild and will continue to do so. Nox will head up our armies and making sure that everyone is ready for if they return here. As for you, you are free to stay here for as long as you want and are free to come and go with your mates. I would like to keep us all close together until this is taken care of." Lord Drake smiled at us.

"We will gladly stay and help rebuild, or even just come back and forth. Either way, I am almost certain our people will want to offer aid in any way that they can." Damian offered. My father smiled at him and nodded his head. Dear gods, he was my father. That was going to take some getting used to. The door opened once more, the blonde woman from earlier entered the room, stopping short and giving a slight bow of the head.

"Ah, Miriam. Is everything okay?" my father asked her.

"Her highness is getting impatient, your Majesty. I fear she may start throwing hands at Carter if he doesn't let her out of the throne room." She bowed, and he laughed.

"Okay, tell her we are coming and let Carter leave his post. I don't need him losing an eye or a hand. Luna, shall we then? I don't feel like having your mother come in here and bring a hurricane with her." He laughed and stood up. We all stood and followed him out of the room and down the hall.

"We got you," Valyn said in my ear. He kissed my cheek. Bastian and Damian grabbed my hands and kissed them.

I smiled at them. I was so nervous but excited. It felt like it took forever for us to make our way to the throne room. I took a deep breath as we stopped in front of the door to the throne room. Hildaria's insignia was engraved on this door as well. The sunlight shined through the stained-glass windows, casting colors and shadows on the floor. I was just glad the sun decided to rise for us at all.

A tall, handsome man who looked to be in his third decade of life was standing outside the doorway, bowing at my father. His eyes were a shade of deep jade and his hair, from what I could see, looked like the night sky itself. He nodded at Nox, then to the princes at my side.

"Carter, you are free to go. See if Bethany needs a hand with some of the elderly patients." My father said and Carter nodded, leaving the door and retreating down the hallway. "Go ahead Luna, she's waiting for you just inside. We will wait out here." Lord Drake smiled and moved out of the way. I kissed each of my mates, then gave Fennik, Niklaus and Virgil a smile as I passed them. Nox stopped me and pulled me into a hug.

"I'm finally glad you know the truth. Welcome home little sis." He smiled and let go of me, stepping back out of the way.

I took a deep breath and looked at my mates as they came to my side. Here goes nothing. I turned the handle on the door and walked into the room.

CHAPTER 46
LUNA

Pacing back and forth at the edge of the dais was the woman identical to me, her eyes the same chocolate brown, her hair an icy snow white. She smiled at me, and I knew at that moment exactly who she was. She moved down the dais and came towards me, stopping short in the middle of the room. Her smile grew as she came closer to me. I stepped through the door, leaving my mates, friends, and family out in the hallway, tears filling my eyes.

I glanced back at Bastian, Valyn and Damian as they stayed outside the doorway watching me, then glancing back toward the beautiful woman across the floor from me. I could tell they were hesitant, but they eventually smiled at me. With those smiles, I took off running across the room. She moved again, meeting me at the halfway point, gathering me in a tight embrace. We sobbed in each other's arms; I didn't know where she began, and I ended. It has been ten long years since she held me, ten long years since I heard her voice, and ten long years without telling my mom that I love her.

I opened my mouth, but she beat me to it. "I've missed you, my little bunny."

"I've missed you too, mom." I hugged her once more, nice and tight. I didn't want to let her go. I feared that if I did, she would vanish again. How in the world could I have forgotten the nickname she gave me to me as a kid? My heart thumped loudly in my chest.

My father walked up behind me and rested his hand on my shoulder. "Can I get one of those too?" He held his arms out, waiting patiently for us to embrace him.

I smiled and grabbed him, pulling them both into a long embrace. They held me tightly. So, this is what a family embrace really was. The guys all walked up to us but stopped just short of reaching us. Today was the hardest but the best day of my life. I got my mom back. I got my mates, but best of all, I got my true family. My mother smiled at me once more.

"Welcome home, Luna." She whispered in my ear and tears streamed down my face. My mates and my newfound brother closed the distance between us, surrounding me and my parents.

"Today has been challenging. I'm just glad we're all here in one piece." Nox said to us all.

I looked over at Virgil and smiled at him. He smiled back at me. We both have grown. Maybe not how we expected our lives to go but, this was definitely a better alternative.

"Luna, I don't mean to be a downer on this but, we still have a problem." Valyn said, trying not to make it obvious who the problem was.

"Luther was riding General Rothsberg. How in the hell did we not know he was a dragon?" Bastian exclaimed, glancing over at Nox.

"I don't know. I never saw him change until today. I always thought he was a rider, not a dragon himself. But it explains a few things. He never took a dragon with him when he left for long journeys. I just assumed his dragon didn't enjoy being around others. Most dragons didn't like crowds. Too much noise and chatter." Nox stated.

"We will figure it out. For now, Hildaria is safe and so is Mirith. The people know that war was not something we wanted or that the King declared. King Harold and I will address the public as soon as he arrives." My father spoke to everyone, and it was final. My mother smiled at me and held my hand. I didn't want to leave yet. I want to speak with my mom more and fill her in on the last ten years. As if sensing where my thoughts were heading, Damian leaned into me.

"Later, my love. Today is the beginning of forever. Don't forget that." Damian whispered in my ear. I looked at my mates, my brother, my friend and my family.

"You're right, here's too forever." I smiled at them all and turned to hug my mom tighter. "Let's go home."

THANK YOU FOR READING!

Thank you so much for reading A Realm of War and Rain. Reviews are vital to authors and help others find our books. I would greatly appreciate it if you could take a moment to leave a review on Amazon and Goodreads, it would mean the world to me!

The war continues in....

A Realm of Fire and Earth (Book 2)

Acknowledgments

Writing this book has been an amazing journey and I am so glad that I had the friends and family who cheered me on.

I want to give a special thanks to those individuals who have sup-ported me.

First of all I want to thank my boyfriend J.D for helping me get some peace and quiet to be able to write and edit and giving me the freedom and space to be myself.

Secondly, a BIG thank you to one of my best friends Jessica for legit being my go to when it came to writing this book,
she let me bounce ideas off her at all hours of the day and I could not be more thankful for her.

I want to thank my sister Victoria and another of my best friends Deb for their amazing reactions to the first reads.

Lastly, I want to thank my boss Jesse for allowing me to do most of my writing at work in between cuts.

Thank you to every friend and family who beta read this book and gave me the feedback I needed to make it better for all to enjoy. You all are definitely the best and I can't express it enough.

About the Author

Krystal Harding is a devoted mother, a full-time barber with the ambitions of becoming a full-time author. She loves to write fantasy, romance (fantasy and dark) and epic fantasy with epic world building and a vast wealth of enchantment and adventure throughout all of her books. When she isn't working or writing more, she can be found reading or making stuff for her books or her shop. She is a gamer, a writer, a mother and a creative mind fueled on caffeine and fantasy realms.

Her inspiration come from years of falling into different worlds through books and movies from Dragonlance to Dungeons and Dragons, from folklore and mythology to the magical worlds of old. Krystal grew up, like most elder millennials, on The Lord of The Rings trilogy, Harry Potter, Eragorn, The Vampire Diaries and Twilight. Krystal loved also finding books and movies that others didn't know about or didn't like.

Her love and passion for reading started at a young age and flourished over the years. She instills the importance of reading onto her children, teaching them that while some games can teach lessons, books teach many more.

Connect with Krystal

Website: www.authorkrystalharding.com

IG, TikTok and Threads @krystal.harding.author

Or on her Facebook Author Krystal Harding

Join the community at Krystal's Korner

ALSO BY

Cerulia

A Realm of Wind and Rain

A Realm of Fire and Earth

A Realm of Flowers and Light

Book 4 coming soon

Seven Deadly Sins

The Book of Wrath

Book 2 coming soon